Ex-detective Taylor Hamilton is broken. After the devastating loss of his children and parents, his marriage crumbled and fell apart. Besides the grief, he is tortured daily by intense pain after a job related shooting. Not willing to face the reality of what his life has become, he finds a way to deal with it that could make everything worse.

Allison Brennan has one huge reason for returning to her childhood home of Laurel Creek, Montana...Taylor Hamilton. Looking for a fresh start after a failed relationship, Allison opens a flower shop and sets her sights on the ex-detective she's loved since high school. Unfortunately the main obstacle in the way is none other than Taylor Hamilton himself.

Do Taylor and Allison have a second chance at love, or will they destroy each other in the process?

BROKEN: TAYLOR

Laurel Creek Series

USA Today Bestselling Author

HILDIE
MCQUEEN

Broken: Taylor

**USA Today Bestselling Author
Hildie McQueen**

Pink Door Publishing

Editor: Dark Dreams Editing

ALSO BY HILDIE McQUEEN

CHAPTER ONE

"I T'S OVER. WE'RE not doing this again Taylor Hamilton." Felicia's barely held rage emanated through the gritted words. She slid from the bed stalking to the dresser.

Her lean, sinewy body, strong and slick with sweat, caught his attention. Disregarding Taylor, she darted about gathering her discarded clothing. The night before had been great, and the sex, totally physical, as always hit the right spot.

However, this morning after another round of sex, passion and want, the mood was replaced by something totally different. Anger, even disappointment perhaps.

The female police detective gave him a flat stare. "This has been a mistake from the beginning. I don't know why we even keep hooking up."

"I don't do weddings. Why is it such a big deal?" Taylor sat up in the bed, his back against the headboard.

It was surprising that he couldn't see his breath when he huffed. The damn hotel room was like a meat locker

1

that morning. Taylor pulled the blanket up across his chest. He'd hoped to stay under the blankets for a couple hours longer. Judging by how things were going, he decided it was best to get up.

Eyes narrowed, Felicia closed the distance between them. Pointing her index finger at his face, she shook her head. "It's not just the wedding. It's everything. I give no damns about the wedding. It's that fucking self entitlement vibe you've got going lately."

Not sure where the conversation was going, he blew out a breath. "You didn't have to come here."

"Your ass could have driven the extra half hour to my house."

"I have to get up early. I've told you that. Plus, I don't want to be around if your family pops up. It would give the wrong message."

Felicia threw her hands up in the air not seeming to care she was totally nude. "Oh. My. God."

Instead of waiting for the explosion that was sure to come, he rolled to the other side of the bed and grabbed his jeans. Just as he yanked them on, Felicia stalked back toward him.

The first slap sent his face sideways, the second made his eyes cross.

"Kiss my ass Taylor Hamilton. I wouldn't bring you around my family."

Noting the telltale shine of unshed angry tears, guilt punched him in the gut.

They'd never made a commitment to each other.

Their relationship consisted of hooking up a couple, sometimes three, times a month. It was sex only. That was the agreement.

Felicia and he had been partners up until he left the force. After he'd retired, they'd met on occasion for lunch or to shoot the bull. One night it changed, and since then they'd gotten together every so often. Mostly for sex.

Today she was angry. Something was up. Yes, he'd promised to come to her place, and then the next day to a wedding, but had decided against it at the last minute. Usually Felicia would have taken it in stride and not made such a big deal about it.

She was dealing with something and he was the easiest, closest target or letting out her frustration.

Before she could turn away, he grabbed her arm. "What's really going on here? What happened?"

Her eyes shifted and shoulders fell. "I shot someone yesterday. Damn it. I killed a damn teenager." Shrugging off his hold, she began yanking on her clothes. "Stupid punks think they are immortal."

The first time he'd killed someone, it was during his second year as a police officer. The time he'd shot an armed robber. At first Taylor had been satisfied because he'd saved the convenience store clerk's life. But when they'd removed the robber's mask to reveal the face of a dumb kid, his guts had been in knots for weeks.

He pulled Felicia against his chest ignoring her struggles until finally she went limp, her tears wet on his bare skin. "When you go and meet up with the shrink, be honest. Don't hold back. I know it seems stupid, but it'll help."

"Shit." Felicia pushed away, wiping at the tears. "I better go." Her dark brown eyes met his for a long moment. "Sorry about the slap. You're a good man, Taylor Hamilton. Give yourself a chance to meet the right woman and settle down."

"You got a hell of a swing. It was two slaps."

Taylor studied the pretty woman. Hopefully she wasn't about to suggest a relationship between them. There was nothing in him to give and he wasn't about to allow anyone, including Felicia, to settle for him.

She was young and beautiful. Had just turned thirty-four. Smart and a go-getter, she had a bright future ahead of her. He was glad she'd not grown to want more from him. The last thing she needed was to be saddled with a forty-six-year-old broken man.

"Hey." He took her arm and tipped her face up to meet his gaze. "I am sorry about being selfish and shit. You deserve better...."

"Get ahold of yourself Hoss. I don't want more from this...from you. We are and will always be friends. But this." She motioned toward the bed. "This part is over."

"Okay. Yeah. As long as we continue to be friends I'm cool with that." Relieved they could always be frank and upfront Taylor hugged her again.

Both finished dressing while talking about the week ahead. It was as if a cloud lifted and they were back to being partners, friends.

"See you around Hamilton." Felicia picked up her overnight bag and walked to the door.

Three weeks later

THE HOUSE WAS too quiet. Tobias, his roommate and cousin, was gone. That morning it was just Taylor and the noisy silence of an empty house. Although there were two dogs in the house, the dogs were probably still asleep.

The clicking sounds from whatever appliance may as well have been a snare drum, the sound emanating from the kitchen into Taylor's bedroom.

Even with a forearm across his eyes and the pillow cushioning his ears, the clicks and occasional sound of a toilet's water running made him want to scream.

Silence normally didn't bother him. However, on mornings when his entire body came to life with blinding pain, every sound pinged directly to the left side of his body. The shattered fragments of his hip that had been pieced together by some talented surgeon never did come to an agreement and work in conjunction. Instead the fuckers staged a daily parade of pain and agony up and down his leg.

Taylor groaned and turned to his right side in hopes of relieving any pressure to the throbbing left hip.

While the damn aches hip-hip-hurrahed in his honor, Taylor clenched his jaw and moaned.

There were only four pain pills left. The next refill

would not be available until later that week. The promise of relief killed any thought of saving some pills for the next couple days.

Carefully avoiding moving his left leg as much as possible, he reached into the nightstand drawer.

Without looking, he grabbed the plastic pill jar and popped the lid off. He couldn't take them all. The prescribed dosage was one, two at the most in one day.

Yeah, like that would do a damned thing.

The lid bounced on the floor and tipping the jar up, three pills slid into his mouth. He saved one for later.

The last thing he needed was to become a prescription drug addict on top of everything else. At least that's what he told himself. As of late, the one-month dosage only lasted half the time.

He maneuvered the pills under his tongue. They would work faster that way. In about fifteen minutes, he could get up, probably not pain free, but with enough of an edge off to make it through another day.

One hour and two cups of coffee later, Taylor was about as ready as he could be to face the day.

It was still early, not quite eight in the morning. However, work could not wait. There was much to do and not enough time for it. The two ranch hands would be there soon, so he didn't worry about the horses being let out to the corrals. However, there were cows to check on and several new additions to the herd that needed tending.

Tobias was gone for two weeks. First week, he'd gone

on vacation with his sister and parents. The second week, he and Luke were going to a ranching convention in Billings.

His aunt and uncle had invited Taylor to go on the cruise with them, insisting they could let one of the ranch hands cover the work.

Oh hell naw. Each time they'd brought it up, he'd declined.

The last thing he needed at the moment was to be in close quarters with anyone. It would be too hard to keep from letting them know how hard things had become lately.

In a way, he was on a vacation of his own. Not having to put up a front, to make excuses for being slow to do things, or his continuous bad temper.

Tobias' dogs, two tan Labradors, trotted to the front door and he opened it to let them out. He was glad for the company, although the dogs preferred being outdoors, which he didn't blame them for.

Bursting with fall colors, the scenery outside made Taylor hesitate and take it all in. Trees of differing heights, rolling hills, and land for as far as he could see with the backdrop of snow-capped mountains was breathtakingly beautiful.

Just over a hill to the left, was where his other cousin, Luke, lived with his girlfriend Leah. However, to see the house, he'd have to go about half a mile out to the edge of the property.

The dogs raced back inside and stood by their food

bowls with expectant expressions.

"Your wish is my command," Taylor mumbled, getting out the dog food and scooping out kibbles.

Just as he placed the full bowls down, the doorbell rang. Chaos ensued.

Bark. Bark. Bark.

Bang. Bang. Bang.

Bark. Bang. Bark. Bang. Tails wagging, the dogs ran in delighted circles by the front door.

Taylor blew out a breath and stared at the door without moving.

"Hey." His cousin Eric and police officer walked in. Dressed in uniform with radio crackling on his shoulder, the guy reminded him of his past. Eric was his aunt's son. Eric and his brother Ernest, the local defense attorney, both lived in Laurel Creek.

Just as tall as him, but with less gray hair, the guy was in peak physical shape. Although in Eric's case, it was all gym since there was little to no crime in Laurel Creek.

Eric petted the dogs and then without asking went straight to the kitchen and opened the cabinet.

The happy dogs raced back to their breakfast.

"Come on in. Make yourself at home," Taylor said, tracking his cousin's movements. "Why'd you even knock? You made the dogs crazy."

Eric ignored him and poured coffee into a chipped cup. "Came by cause I was just up the street. Seems the Davis' daughter ran away. Seen or heard anything last night?"

Even if fireworks had exploded outside, he would have slept right through it thanks to his pills.

The girl was trouble. Always up to something or another. Although he didn't know the family well, they seemed like normal, nice folks. Taylor wondered why the girl was so desperate to get away.

"Just got up. We can go check the stables if you want. I haven't heard anything."

Eyes narrowed, Eric moved closer to Taylor. "What's wrong with your eyes?"

"Just took my pain pills a bit ago."

"How many?"

Shit, the last thing he needed was his cop cousin deciding to be nosy. "One. The normal dosage."

"Bull. Shit."

"I thought you were here to look for a girl. Get out of my face."

Of course the asshole didn't budge. "When was the last time you went to the doctor? Have you been to the pain clinic?"

He'd stopped going. It was a waste of time and the last thing he had time for was to waste it. "Last week."

"Bull. Shit."

"Will you stop saying it like that? It's bullshit. One word."

Instead of replying, Eric lifted his cell phone up and punched in a number. "Hey Louis, this is Eric Hamilton. Do you have an opening for Taylor Hamilton? He needs to come in today if possible."

"I'm not going."

"Two o'clock is fine. He'll be there."

"I'm not going. There is too much shit to do around here. Tobias is gone. You want to go out there and explain to the cows why they're not getting fed?"

Eric lifted a shoulder. "I get off at three, I'll come give you a hand." Eric's index finger pressed into his left shoulder. "You're going to see the doctor. If I have to punch your lights out and drag you there, so be it."

"Yeah, like that's going to happen."

Taylor decided to let the discussion go for the moment. "I'll go with you to check the stables. Other than that, I don't know where else the girl could hide. Maybe the old cabin."

THE AIR ON his face was just what he needed. Taylor's four-wheeler crested a small hill and his great-great-grandfather's cabin came into view. The home had once belonged to Marcus Hamilton, his namesake. It was the only structure that remained mostly intact.

Although his family called him Taylor, his first name was actually Marcus. His mother had always called him by his middle name and it had stuck.

Eric came up on his right. "Think someone's in there?"

"Nah. The door is hard to open and unless she's industrious, there is nothing in there that makes it remotely accommodating."

"This window is broken," Eric said inspecting a small side window. "Didn't Tobias empty it not too long ago?"

Taylor nodded. "Nope. He hates snakes and a mama snake decided it was the perfect home for her family." It was hard not to laugh at the memory of Tobias running out and doing some sort of freak-out dance after spotting the nest of snakes.

They pulled up and cut off the engines. Taylor allowed Eric to go first. Although he'd medically retired from law enforcement, he was not in the mood to play cop.

"Stay back," Eric said, holding his hand up. "Someone's in there." The change in his cousin was obvious. All cop. He put his hand on his weapon and stood to the side of the door. "Police. Come out."

THE PERPETRATOR TURNED out to be a raccoon, which wasn't at all impressed by Eric's tone. They decided to let it be and turned back to the stables.

Taylor could tell by his cousin's grim face, the guy was worried about the girl.

"You know at sixteen, she's old enough to know better. If the girl wants to disappear and not be found, there isn't much that can be done.

"I know. Just hate to go back and tell the parents she's gone. My guess is she probably left in the middle of the night. Someone had to have picked her up. She could be anywhere by now."

"I better get on." Eric met Taylor's gaze for a long beat. "Go to that appointment."

Taylor nodded, knowing he'd call and cancel. So yeah, he had to go eventually and be seen so that the prescription would be refilled. However, he'd go when it suited him.

CHAPTER TWO

THE STRONG COFFEE did little to sooth her already frazzled nerves. Allison Brennan's hand shook as she lifted the cup to her lips. Her over active imagination had kept her up way too late. It was hard being a night owl in the normal world.

Most nights, she struggled to go to sleep before one in the morning, but last night, one a.m. had come and went. By the time she fell asleep, it was closer to three in the morning.

In her estimation, by mid afternoon she'd be useless and in dire need of a nap.

Sometimes in the middle of the night, she'd wake up freaked out. Every possible scenario of what could go wrong with her life or anyone who she loved would take over. And after tossing and turning for hours, she always gave up and got out of bed.

The early morning was a series of check up calls and lurking on social media to make sure everyone was all right.

Jaden, her twenty-two-year-old stepson, always answered the phone by the third ring. Used to her occasional early morning calls, Jaden's groggy voice always assured her. He'd wave away her apologies for waking him and ensure he'd fall right back to sleep. Knowing him, he would.

Although Allison got married too young and was not prepared for it, she'd enjoyed helping to raise her ex-husband's young son. Even after an amicable divorce, she'd ensured to be a constant in Jaden's life.

AFTER DOUBLE-CHECKING HER bank account balances, and ensuring no one had broken into the shop and stolen everything she owned, the doubt of something unforeseen or that she'd missed an ominous sign would continue to bother her until at least two cups of coffee were downed.

Unfortunately, the day ahead always ended up being a total waste. With lack of sleep came irritability and absence of focus.

This morning, she'd already called Jaden, checked the accounts, and every room in her grandmother's old house.

After walking through the bottom floor of the house where her flower and gift shop was located, she trudged upstairs to the kitchen to pour another cup of coffee.

The warm cup between her palms soothed Allison as she went to stand by a window, which looked over Broad

Street in downtown Laurel Creek, Montana.

Through the glass, she had a view of the entire street and on past to the outskirts of town, where the road disappeared from view.

Although it was nine o'clock in the morning, the center of town was strangely quiet.

The boutique across the way had not opened yet and next to it, the small pizzeria's blinds were still down.

A car and a truck were parked in front of the coffee shop, the only place with the lighted "Open" sign.

Fresh air blew in through the window when she slid it open, the singing of birds filling the air. It would be a perfect time to meditate, read her devotional, or do the yoga exercises she was supposed to do on mornings like this.

Her shop didn't open until ten, so she took advantage of the early rise to make her bed, put a load of laundry into the washer, and tidy up the bathroom.

AN HOUR LATER, dressed in jeans and an off one shoulder pale peach top, Allison pulled her wavy hair up into a messy bun that allowed curls to escape and frame her face. She swiped a couple of coats of mascara on and did the same with a sheer coral lip-gloss.

Cup of coffee in hand, she went downstairs to open her shop noting a large truck had pulled up.

She opened the door just as the deliveryman walked up to the front porch with a large item on a hand truck.

"I've got your sign," the heavyset bearded man mumbled and held up a clipboard.

Her new business sign had arrived.

"Can we unwrap it so I can see it please?" There was a strange bright orange colored corner poking out, but the rest was covered with cardboard and packing tape.

The more the man uncovered, the worse it got. The sign was horrendous.

"The Flower Pot" in bright neon green letters on an even brighter orange background was not exactly what the website had shown. It definitely did not fit the theme for her shop.

Obviously the computer had done an amazing job of making the colors look very different. Allison leaned back, shaded her eyes and looked at the sign.

She scrunched up her face. "That is the ugliest thing I've ever seen."

The deliveryman was honest enough to nod. "It'll definitely stand out."

"Ya think?" Allison laughed. "If it wasn't so darn expensive, I would take a hammer to it."

By the way the man shuffled from one foot to the other, he either had to use the bathroom or was hoping to get away before she decided to ask him to take it back.

"I suppose I can paint over the letters or outline them in black." It was a lie. Nothing she could do herself would fix the monstrous colors. "I have to return it. I'm sorry. I'll be right back." She rushed inside to get her cell before the man could stop her.

The phone on the other end rang at least five times before a woman answered and asked her to hold for a few moments while they retrieved her order.

Through the window, a new annoyance came into view. Taylor Hamilton walked up to the deliveryman and they exchanged greetings. So, Taylor knew the guy. Interesting.

Taylor then looked to the front porch and his eyebrows lifted. He nodded at something the delivery guy said. At least the ugly sign was sure to attract attention if she was forced to keep it.

Damn the man was so good looking. Wisps of gray at his temples added a sensual maturity to the already hot country boy. He'd always been about fitness and sports, but he'd certainly filled out nicely in all the right places over the years.

A jock in high school, everyone had expected him to go into sports. Instead, while in college on a football scholarship, he'd studied criminal justice and joined the Billings police department right after graduation. Until recently, he'd been living there.

The ex-cop seemed to sense her regard and his hazel gaze met hers through the glass. His lips did not curve in greeting, instead he gave a subtle nod.

Queue the idiotic butterflies in her stomach. Of course, she smiled widely and waved.

What a lunatic.

Could she be more obvious? She might as well have ordered a second sign with the words *"I moved to Laurel*

Creek in hopes I can have a relationship with Taylor Hamilton."

The woman at the sign company took pity and gave her instructions for a return. Thankfully, they seemed to understand the reason for the return and would give her credit for a new one. Allison took a deep breath and walked out to give the deliveryman the message and return confirmation number.

Just as she exited the shop, Taylor left. He didn't look back, nor did he seem particularly interested in making it apparent how fast he rushed away.

Her gaze lingered on his butt before she turned to the deliveryman. "You know Taylor huh?"

"Yeah, we played together in a city league years back."

Taylor's truck peeled away from the curb and down the road. "Wonder what the rush is?"

The delivery guy gave a one-shoulder shrug.

Men were dumbasses.

IT WOULD PROBABLY be a while before customers came to browse, so Allison took advantage of the lull and hustled across the street to the coffee shop.

Mindy Clark, the owner of Cuppa Joe, was from the neighboring town, but had moved to Laurel Creek a few years earlier. She looked up and smiled. "Hey there Allie. Good morning."

Mindy was always in a good mood. Allison wondered

if after hours, she went home and kicked her cat or something. It was doubtful, as Mindy seemed to genuinely enjoy her life.

"Did you finally get the shop sign? I saw a delivery truck pull up?" Mindy asked while steaming milk for a latte.

Allison huffed. "It was hideous I had to send it back. Lost a hundred bucks for shipping and stuff, but it's worth it."

"You shouldn't have to pay for their mistake." Tori, a pretty brunette had just entered and Allison hugged her.

Tori, she and Leah, who lived in Laurel Creek as well, had once been very close. However, they'd all gone to separate colleges and as expected she and Tori had not seen much of each other since.

Now that Allison was back in town and Tori worked at her small pizzeria across the street, they were becoming reacquainted.

Plenty of conversation and a toasted bagel sandwich later, Allison hurried back across the street to open up shop.

Her shop was an oasis. Fresh cut flowers and aromatic teas formed a soothing combination. The entwined fragrances were a perfect greeting for customers.

It was hard to remain stressed or uptight when surrounded by the beauty of flowers like roses, lilies, or carnations and the prospect of a delicious cup of tea.

The ambiance was finished off with soft spa like

music from hidden speakers.

The serene atmosphere of her new shop suited Allison perfectly. Even after the sleepless night, ugly sign episode, and Taylor Hamilton's appearance, she felt calm and relaxed.

Thank goodness she'd found a love of flowers after her divorce. Amidst the days of feeling adrift, Allison took a flower arranging night class to fill the time. From that instruction, she discovered a gift for it. Months later her talent became a way to earn a living while doing something she loved.

Sure, there were times when shipments were late or a bride had a meltdown. These issues could make her job stressful. However, for the most part, flowers were all about special occasions.

Whether it was a happy or sad circumstance, the presence of flowers brightened people's days.

The bell over the door jingled as her best friend Leah walked in. Ever since moving to Laurel Creek and getting together with Taylor's cousin, Luke, Leah was in a perpetual glowing from the inside mode. Allison chalked it up to regular doses of good lovemaking.

Even now, her friend's lips were curved into what could only be described as a satisfied smile.

"Hi," Leah said, immediately distracted by the new display of chocolate truffles. "Ooh. I forgot you were getting these."

Allison laughed. "Yeah right. Then why are you in town so early?"

"I'll have you know Luke and I decided to have a

breakfast date before he left for Billings."

Was that the reason Taylor was in town as well? "Who all is going?"

"Luke and Tobias. Tobias is leaving from his vacation trip with the family and meeting Luke in Billings. Taylor is staying behind to take care of the ranch. Besides, Luke says he's been a bear to be around lately. Probably needs to be alone."

It was hard to imagine Luke calling anyone a bear, especially since Luke wasn't exactly the most easygoing of guys.

"What's up with Taylor? He was here in town earlier. Didn't say much, just nodded and high-tailed it."

Judging by her scowl, Leah was pondering how much to say. When her friend shrugged, it meant she'd unload an entire shipment of four-one-one.

"It's the anniversary of his kids and ex-in-laws' accident." Leah let out a long sigh. "And I guess his ex wants him to come to Wyoming and pick up some boxes. She's ready to move on or something and wants him to take the kids' stuff she's keeping. Seems that Taylor never dealt with all the belongings and she's been storing them."

"I can't imagine," Allison said walking to the truffle display. "They lost both kids and her parents at the same time in a car accident. How devastating."

She took a pink-topped truffle out and placed it on a small marble board. After carefully cutting it in half, she held out one part to Leah. "We can't test them all, I'll go broke."

"We can always order more," Leah mumbled between chews. "Oh."

Allison had to admit, the confection was delicious. "We?"

"I'll pay for a truckload. Imagine these with a glass of cabernet."

"We're going to be chubby drunk chicks with rotten teeth." Allison frowned as she considered a second one.

"True," Leah agreed. "I feel horrible about what happened to Taylor's children and in-laws. And then there was the follow-up of his marriage ending and the bank shooting that cost him his career. It's all so tragic. I wish there was something we could do."

"Poor guy, how horrible," Allison agreed.

Her friend pointed to another truffle and she obliged. "Oh and his mom is in prison for life. You knew that, didn't you?"

Allison nodded. "I remember it happened after he arrived here. We all thought he came because his parents were moving to Laurel Creek, but it turned out his mom planned it so that he'd be gone when she killed his dad."

"Yeah, that was crazy." Leah shuddered. "She was hoping to cash the life insurance or something."

LEAH LEFT WITH six truffles just as two women walked in. By the quick scans and the look of utter dismay on the younger one's face, it was obvious they were a mother and bride to be.

Allison had been in the business long enough to know how to recognize them.

"Hello ladies. How about we start off with a cup of tea and discuss what you're up to today."

The older woman sighed. "That sounds lovely, but I don't know if we have time. We need to show you pictures and get an estimate for flowers before heading to a luncheon."

"I have some ideas," the bride, who looked to be in her mid-twenties said, holding up a thick binder. "My wedding colors are buttercream and chocolate."

Why did brides insist on naming their color choices after food? If and when she got remarried, there would be no color theme whatsoever.

Allison steered them to a table with four chairs. "Sounds great, let's talk." While they settled and placed magazines and the binder on the surface of the glass table, she poured two cups of lavender chamomile tea.

It was almost comical. Both immediately picked up their cup and took a sip and at the same time slow smiles curved their lips. Yes, as always, chamomile tea was magical.

By the time the women left, both were satisfied with her suggestions. Not only had she urged the bride into a contrasting color, which the mother wanted to add, but also, she'd helped them design a cake around the theme.

Her cell buzzed and she picked it up while waving to a new customer.

"Can you go by Taylor's and tell him to answer his

damn phone?" Luke sounded frustrated. "I tried to ask Leah, but she's gone to a meeting with her dad."

"I can go by there this afternoon," Allison replied, already thinking that perhaps she could get someone else to go.

Luke grunted. "Okay. That'll work. I need to get some information from him tonight before making some decisions."

"You guys don't have a landline?" Allison asked. A lot of people in the area still had landlines.

She could hear Luke ask his brother. "Yeah there is, but they don't have a phone hooked up to it."

"Thanks, I appreciate it. He can use your phone if you don't mind. But I need to talk to him."

After they ended the call, Allison decided it was best to go sooner than later. She quickly helped the customer with a bouquet so she could go find Taylor. It sounded as if they really did need to talk to Taylor. She grabbed her purse and light jacket.

Allison studied her reflection in the antique mirror she'd hung by the door. It was good to check one's appearance before leaving.

Not that it mattered how she looked. Allison was pretty sure she could show up dressed in a prison uniform and cornrows without Taylor blinking an eye.

Taylor was not interested in her, or dating anyone as far as she'd heard. He'd stopped by just a few weeks earlier and ordered flowers. It seemed he was still hung up on his ex-wife.

CHAPTER THREE

THE GATE TO the Hamilton lands was rarely closed and that day was no exception. Allison drove through the opening, guiding her late model light green Prius toward the house. Taylor was probably at the stables, but if she went to the house first and he was not there, she could claim to have tried to find him. She'd leave a big note so he'd know to call his cousins.

The ranch house was a beautiful log cabin with a wide front porch that spanned the entire length of it. On the spacious front area, there were a couple of rockers on one side and a swing on the other.

Luke and Tobias' mother had often decorated according to the seasons. Allison remembered on several occasions when visiting the family with her mother, she'd hung out on the porch with either of the twins.

Between Luke and Tobias, Tobias was the more easygoing of the two and also the one whom she was closer to.

Back then, in her early teens, the last thing on her

mind was dating or flirting. If anything, she found the twins annoying and stinky. It all changed when Taylor came to spend the summer during their sophomore year. Since his parents were planning to move to Laurel Creek, they had sent Taylor ahead so he could get to know the kids around there and start school. Of course, things had turned out horribly, and Taylor had ended up living with his cousins.

The first time she'd seen him, he rode up on a bicycle, dropped it on the ground and rushed inside the house. He'd not paid her the slightest attention, and Allison had been relieved. She'd barely been able to form a thought, much less speak.

That night she'd gone to bed thinking of the cute boy who lived with the Hamiltons and couldn't wait for school to start so she could see him regularly.

ENOUGH WITH THE musings, she had to let Taylor know to call his cousins. After digging around, she found a notepad in her glove compartment and wrote a quick note instructing Taylor to call them. Satisfied no one was about, she got out of the car and hurried to the front door.

Guilt assailed her as she wondered if he'd see the note. What if he was already inside and didn't see it until morning?

It wasn't as if she was in awe of him like back in high school. It was more that at the moment, they were at a strange impasse of sorts. They'd not had a disagreement per se, more of an uncomfortable occurrence.

Taylor had been at her shop to order flowers for his ex-wife. She'd gone to stand beside him as he chose the bouquet on her laptop.

She'd turned to look at him, and he'd responded by staring back. One thing led to another, and they'd made out right in the center of her flower shop.

Just as they were about to head up the stairs to make the mistake even worse, a customer had walked in. Taylor had practically run out the door.

After that, they'd avoided each other.

So mature.

"Are you going to knock or just stand there?"

Allison screamed and the dogs that accompanied Taylor broke out barking. He'd walked up and she'd not heard him. Too busy musing.

So, while the dogs circled them, wagging tails and jumping, both she and Taylor did their best to look anywhere but at each other.

"Luke and Tobias have been trying to reach you all day." She finally met his hazel gaze. "They need to talk to you before making a decision about something. You haven't been answering your cell."

His right hand went to his back pocket and then to his front jeans pocket. "Damn. Where did I leave that thing?"

She looked past him to his truck. "Truck?"

"Right. Hold up." He signaled for her to wait and

went to the silver truck. While he rummaged through the vehicle, she crossed her arms and waited.

Finally he came back to the porch. "Not in there. Can't imagine leaving it anywhere else."

She followed him into the house and was astounded by how pristine it was. From the entryway, there was what looked to be an office to the right and a dining room on the left. The furnishings were obviously high end, and she surmised had been left from when Taylor's aunt and uncle lived there.

They continued into a spacious living room and kitchen combination. Even there, everything was in its place. There were comfortable leather couches with plush throws over one arm. Two recliners flanked on one side with tall tables perfect for holding a laptop and cup of coffee were centered facing the fireplace.

"Your house is incredible." She couldn't help walking into the center of the room to take in the décor. "That's amazing," she said, pointing to a metal modern art fixture above the fireplace.

Taylor looked to the piece. "My aunt decorated the place. We have a weekly cleaning service, so you can't give us credit for it staying like this."

"With two bachelors living here, I expected open pizza boxes and dirty underwear on the floor."

His handsome face scrunched into a look of disgust. "That would be gross."

"Pizza or the underwear?" Allison enjoyed teasing him.

"I only allow myself that luxury once or twice a month at the most. I am pretty much a chicken and vegetable guy. Dirty underwear is okay."

"Really, that's all you eat?" She scanned his sleek muscular body. "You competing for some sort of body building thing?"

He met her gaze for a long beat until she had to look away. "My stomach is messed up from when I got shot. Had to have my spleen and gall bladder removed and other stuff got rearranged. So I can't eat a lot of the stuff I really like."

"Oh, that makes sense." Allison shrugged not wanting to focus on his body any longer. "You need to find your phone. Or, you can use mine to call the guys."

Taylor walked to the kitchen, looked around and then disappeared down a hall to where she imagined was his bedroom. To keep busy, she went to the recliners and felt around the sides. Coming up empty, she did the same with the couch.

When he returned, she couldn't take her eyes off of him. At the doorway, his height was emphasized. He was well toned, with muscular arms and a broad chest. It had to be a Hamilton trait how well they filled out their jeans. He wore a simple dark t-shirt and unbuttoned plaid short-sleeved shirt over it.

"Shit. I must have dropped it somewhere." He scratched his head. "I've been out on the four-wheeler two days straight. Don't remember the last time I used it."

"I'll go get mine so you can call Tobias," Allison said and headed outside. She took her entire tote bag out of the car and went back inside. Taylor was in the kitchen fiddling with a coffee maker. His gaze moved to hers and quickly away.

They were going to have the conversation he was obviously trying very hard to avoid. It didn't matter what the reason was, Allison needed to know why he high-tailed it every time they ran into each other. So, maybe he'd say because of the ex-wife and his feelings for her or whatever.

It was probably a bad idea to go down that road. But damn it, there was a connection between them. And if she'd gone so far as to move to Laurel Creek to explore what could happen, Allison wasn't about to give up that easily.

For the first time in her life, she was going to take control and stop being the "go with the flow" girl. This time her sights were set on Taylor Hamilton, and she was bound and determined to pull the trigger.

If she'd missed all the signs and it didn't work out, then so be it. At least she'd tried.

"Here ya go. Luke's number is in the recent calls list." She held out the cell phone and leaned back against the counter. "I'll have a cup of coffee while you're at it."

His lips curved and damn if that wasn't a total turn on. Allison cleared her throat. "I'll make coffee," she repeated.

He took the phone and traded places, standing with

his hip against the counter opposite where she stood.

Allison waited for the first cup to fill, keeping her back to him and listening to his end of the conversation.

"I don't know what I did with it."

"When are you seeing the guy again?"

"Yeah."

"I'll go get another phone in the morning."

"What?"

"Yeah."

"Don't wait on me to call. I trust your judgment."

"All right. Yeah, the guys have that covered."

"Bye."

He placed the cell on the counter and looked to the coffee maker.

Allison moved closer until they were but a few inches apart. "You've been avoiding me. Why?"

CHAPTER FOUR

T HE LOST CELL phone was just another of the stupid things he'd done lately. He could blame some of it on the medication. Nothing made sense lately, much less how or why he'd been avoiding the beautiful woman in front of him.

No, that was a lie. Taylor knew exactly why he avoided her. She was too much to take at the moment. Everything about her was perfection. From the locks of soft waves that tumbled past her shoulders, the plump lips that he pictured doing things better left unthought-of at the moment, and her eyes. Like something he'd never seen before. They were like pools of sapphire he could dive into and never come up for air.

Only a fool would walk away from the brink of making love to Allison Brennan. And, he was that fool.

She was the type of woman a man only dreamed of and given the chance would take it. The last two years of high school, he'd watched her every move, often doing crazy stuff just to impress her.

But of course, she was dating some jock, and although friendly, she never gave him a chance.

And now, during the worst time of his life, when he was losing control did he get the opportunity to finally get to know her, be with her. Damn his luck.

"That day...it was not my best. I should have..." Hell what he saying? It was hard to think straight when her fragrance, something soft and citrus like, tickled his nose. "Shit. I don't know what to tell you."

She arched a brow and placed a hand on her hip. "How about the truth. There is obviously something here." She motioned between them with her right hand.

"If you're not interested, then I get it. But the other day, it was you who initiated things."

If she didn't step back, he was going to lose control again. So Taylor walked around her and went for the coffee.

Allison rolled her eyes. "Look, forget it. Do you need to use the phone again? If not, I gotta go."

"Yeah. Thanks."

He first dialed his own number and nothing happened. It rang a few times in his ear and then went to voicemail. He punched in the key code and listened to several messages. There was three from Tobias and one from the pain management center regarding his missed appointment.

He then called the phone provider and after six hundred computer prompts finally spoke to a human.

While he got the details on a new phone and that

they'd deliver it the following day via express mail, Allison stood by the front window peering out.

The dogs were automatically beside her. She looked back to him and he nodded to let her know she could let them out. It wasn't as if they'd go far. It was their dinnertime.

Finally the call ended and he went to where she stood. He did owe her an explanation. But how did he tell her the only way he'd pursue any relationship was once he got his shit straight?

He'd already come close to ruining his friendship with Felicia. His head was messed up with all the pain and pills he'd been forced to take. Everything was going to hell in a hand basket at the moment.

Things with Felicia could be repaired. They would go back to being ex-partners and friends.

With Allison, it was more complicated.

Hell, he didn't even know what his problem was. Between the latest bouts with pain, which seemed worse by the day, and taking so many painkillers that fuzzed the fuck out of his brain, it was a toss up.

"Thank you." He held out the phone, but when she reached for it, he couldn't let it go.

Wide eyes met his and with a sharp intake of breath, she released the hold on the phone. "What?"

He cupped her jaw with the other hand. "You're the most beautiful woman I've ever met. I still can't believe I walked away. I didn't want to. Not sure why I did."

Although her brows came together, she didn't say

anything.

"I don't have anything to give Allison. There's so much shit in my life right now. It would be unfair to push it on you."

An electrical charge traveled through him when her hand covered his.

"Okay." The word was soft and yet there was so much that didn't have to be said. Disappointment, curiosity, and acceptance came through loud and clear.

The pull became too strong. He yanked her against him and covered her mouth with his. Desperate to take as much as he could, Taylor wrapped his arm around her waist and held her while ravaging her mouth.

Although stiff at first, Allison finally softened and she responded to his kiss, her lips parting to allow his tongue into her mouth. She suckled at it. When she wrapped her arms around his neck, victory sang out in his head.

Unlike the time before, there was no excuse this time, nothing to interrupt them.

Sliding his hands down every delectable inch of her curves, he cupped her butt and pulled her closer. Allison moaned when he trailed his tongue down from the corner of her mouth to her neck.

His dick was rock hard and although he wouldn't push things that far, damn if he didn't want Allison on her back with her legs wrapped around his hips.

Instead he took her mouth again and holding her hips, pushed himself into her, the signal clear of what he wanted. It had to be her decision. He'd not push her.

Damn, at this point, he was out of control. She had to call it. Had to stop it.

Although every part of his body screamed to be buried deep in Allison, it would be a huge mistake. He'd only ruin things and lose any chance of a future relationship.

Thankfully, she had more sense than he did. Hands flat on his chest, she pushed away. Cheeks flushed and lips without lipstick now, she was even more beautiful, if that was possible.

"I better go." Breathless, she raked her fingers through her hair. "I should go," she repeated.

Taylor nodded and looked around. What had he done with her cell?

"I took it." Her lips curved into a sweet smile that made his chest tighten. "You were distracted. And, sending totally mixed signals as usual."

"I know. I know." He moved backward, his calf hitting an ottoman. "Sorry about that."

"About what Taylor?" She looked up at the ceiling as if to calm her temper. In actuality, he wanted to see her lose it with him. Not only would it be sexy as all get out, but also maybe she'd keep her distance from then on. It had to be her because damn if he could keep from touching her whenever she was anywhere close.

When he didn't reply, she shook her head. "Just forget it."

Once again, his body reacted without his brain engaging and he reached for her. Allison side-stepped and opened the front door. "Good luck with your phone issue." Her eyes scanned over his face searching for some sort of clue. Good luck there, he had no idea what was going on with him at the moment either.

"You and I will talk." With that statement hanging in the air, she walked out.

The dogs bounded in, tails wagging and their happy faces excited about nothing in particular. He envied them at the moment.

Taylor rushed out to the porch just as Allison was getting into her car. "I'll pick you up for dinner tomorrow. Six."

She frowned and after a few moments nodded.

THERE WAS LITTLE choice in where to go out to eat and so when he asked Allison to dinner it became obvious that no matter where they went, someone would take notice.

He'd caught up with her before she'd left the day before and on pure impulse asked her to dinner. She'd agreed reluctantly, eyes narrowed in suspicion. Probably thought he was joking. Doing the mixed signal thing again.

It was not a joke. It could be another misstep in a long string of mistakes he was making lately. Now as he walked with her to Victoria's, the small pizzeria owned by Tobias' ex girlfriend, he wondered if perhaps they should have gone to Ed's Barbeque or Shooters instead.

Then again, Shooters was not an option. Not only was it loud, but also there was the distinct possibility he wasn't welcome back yet. The last time he was there, he and Luke had gotten into a brawl with some good ol' boys.

Allison was a vision in a green off the shoulder blouse, tight jeans and heels. Immediately his mind went into thoughts wanting those heels to stay on if she ever slept with him.

"I'm starving. It smells so good," Allison said sniffing the air. "Mmmm."

She kept her distance from him as they walked down the sidewalk and when he touched her lower back to guide her into the pizzeria, she stiffened.

"Hey," Tori, the owner and Tobias' ex, met them, her gaze moving from him to Allison. She smiled brightly at Allison. "Hey girl. Long time no see." Some sort of secret message passed between the women and Taylor decided it was best to ignore it.

They settled into a booth at the back wall of the restaurant. Annoying as all get out because as Allison walked past, hips swaying, more than one man took notice. Even when he glared at a couple of the guys, they promptly ignored him and took a second look. Idiots.

"A glass of Merlot please," Allison told the young girl who came to take their order. Taylor ordered a beer while Allison perused the menu.

He pretty much knew it by heart since pizza or pasta

was a weekly occurrence at his house. Her gaze lifted over the menu to meet his. "Want to share a large pizza?"

"I eat it with sauce and vegetables only. No cheese."

"We're not sharing then." Brows pinched she continued looking at the menu.

Taylor studied her for a moment. "Why did you move back here?" Most people move from Laurel Creek to Billings, not the other way around. Unless running from something or planning to retire, there really wasn't much in Laurel Creek.

"It's beautiful here. My best friend is here and besides, I can live here mortgage free in my grandmother's house."

The girl returned and they ordered a medium pizza each, his with vegetables only. Allison ordered a supreme with extra spinach and cheese.

"Why did you ask me out to eat tonight?"

He wasn't sure how to respond. The true reason for them being there was because he owed her some sort of explanation, which by the way he'd not figured out yet.

The only good news so far was that he'd gotten his phone and his prescription refill was safely in his nightstand.

He met her gaze. "Allison, I don't want to be on bad terms with you. Need you to understand that right now I can't promise more than friendship."

"Okay." Without expression, she scanned the room not seeming to notice a guy who sat across from them. The idiot kept turning to look at her.

"So you returned to get a fresh start then?" Taylor asked, attempting at a neutral subject.

Sipping from her wine, she watched him over the rim. "I recently ended a long-term relationship, so the timing was good to move. What about you? What's going on in your life at the moment?"

Shit, his current situation was not the best. Nothing could be done about the daily pain and taking too many painkillers. It wasn't like they could amputate a hip.

"Day to day same thing."

"I was told you go to Billings often. Are you dating someone there? Is it serious?"

So that was the message between Allison and Tori. Tori knew about Felicia, they'd been there for dinner once. After drinking a bit too much wine, they'd gotten a bit demonstrative. Shit. He'd not thought about that.

"I was seeing someone. Not in a relationship currently."

"Breakup must have been recent."

Fuck. The conversation was going from uncomfortable to unbearable. He didn't like talking about his personal life or the shitstorm that it was. "It was a casual thing. Nothing serious."

She emptied her wineglass and gestured for a refill. "Just so we're clear. This is just dinner between friends. Nothing more." She leaned back and let out a breath, her gaze moving past him. He didn't have to wonder who'd caught her attention.

"Its just dinner. Not a date." He gritted the words out. In all honesty, he wanted it to be more. Hell, maybe he was sending mixed signals even to himself at this point. Why did he even ask her out?

Once again, her gaze moved past him and she smiled. "So, are you more of a casual relationship type?"

"Sometimes. You?"

"Not sure."

He took drink from his glass. "Okay. Satisfied? Any more questions?"

The evening was headed downhill.

His phone buzzed. It was Felicia of all people. What the hell?

Allison lifted a brow. "No, I can't say I'm satisfied. But I will be once I eat this little darling." Pizzas were slid in front of both of them and Allison began eating with gusto.

Apparently, she was not fazed by the situation. On the other hand, he could not eat. His cell continued to vibrate and guilt settled in his gut filling up most of the space.

Allison getting up to use the ladies room and the asshole at the other table slipping a piece of paper into her hand topped off the evening.

Taylor blew out a breath and pulled out his cell phone. It was then he looked across the restaurant and noticed Felicia was there. What the hell was she doing there?

So yeah, they'd left on "friends only" terms, but it still felt odd to be out with another woman with her in the same place. And she did have relatives there, but still.

"Shit."

CHAPTER FIVE

ALLISON RETURNED AND looked at his barely touched pizza. "Not hungry?"

"I shouldn't really eat all this. But the one slice I had was great." He tried his best not to look to where Felicia sat with another woman whom he recognized as her cousin.

Had she come to check up on him? Probably not. She had relatives in Laurel Creek and came often.

The town was too damn small.

Allison had obviously pondered what she'd said while gone from the table. "Look forget everything. We don't have to talk about what happened. It's all right. The more I think about it, the more I realize what a mistake it was to think something could develop between us."

She emphasized the words with hand gestures and for a moment he was lost in the bounce of her curls and jingling of bracelets.

Although Felicia was deep in conversation, she kept glancing over. It was obvious she was trying to figure out the situation. Not because of jealousy, but more to size Allison up and decide if she was good enough for him.

They finished the rest of their meal. Their conversation flowed easily, without any more references to what had transpired between them the day before.

Allison even made him laugh several times with stories of contrary customers. He had to admit, she was a delight in more ways than one. Spending time with her this evening almost made him forget the pain and issues from his injuries.

Although he pictured what a relationship would be like with her, it seemed each time a picture of him moaning through the night and barely able to function every morning ruined any illusion. So yeah, in many ways he was an idiot for not pursuing this woman. At the same time, the stark reality was she deserved much more. A whole man.

The boxed up pizza leftovers between them a was sign the meal had definitely ended.

"Thank you for dinner," Allison said stretching.

He slid out of the booth and shrugged on his jacket. While she put her own overcoat on, he took the pizza boxes. "I'll walk you home."

Once outside on the sidewalk, Allison took the top box. Their gazes met for a moment before she looked away first. "Have a good night Taylor. I'll see you around."

Before he could say anything, she pressed a kiss to his cheek.

"Look Allison…"

She shook her head. "Nope. Don't say anything. Like I said, I get it."

A slight drizzle started, the weather adding to the fast descent of his mood as Allison crossed the street and went into her place. He stood planted to the spot until the light upstairs came on.

THE LOUD EXAGGERATED grunt was meant to irritate. Taylor glared at Tobias, who placed the free weights into place and then posed like a super hero. "What do you think? I could be Captain America, right?"

"How about Captain Moron?" Taylor pushed up the next five repetitions ignoring Tobias, who obviously had something to say by the way he hovered.

Taylor finally placed the bar back on the stand and remained laying on the bench to wait on whatever Tobias had to say.

"You okay Cuz?"

"Yep. You?"

"Aren't you supposed to go to Wyoming? To get stuff?"

In this family, not only was it impossible to keep secrets, but they also interfered when one decided to ignore things.

"Yep."

"Janice called Mom. She's pretty angry. Said you

weren't answering her calls."

"My phone was lost for a couple of days. I don't know what the damn hurry is." He gave up and sat. Placing his hands on his thighs, he bent forward and let out a long breath.

Tobias didn't give up. "I can go with you if you want me to. I know you don't want her to get rid of all the stuff before you at least get a chance to look."

His ex-wife had sold their old home and was moving to Canada. Taylor didn't blame her for wanting to move on. As a matter of fact, he was glad for her. But damn if he wasn't sure how to gather the strength to go through what had been their children's belongings.

"I'm sick of all this shit." Taylor got to his feet and stalked to the door. Unfortunately, Tobias was on his heels. When he swung around they almost bumped chests.

Taylor pushed him away. The asshole barely budged. "What is it with everybody suddenly trying to fucking babysit me? I'm a forty-six-year-old man. I don't need this shit. I'll do what I want, when I want."

Of course Tobias was not at all phased by his tirade. "Yeah, so that would be cool if not for the fact others are counting on your ass to get the shit done."

"Janice can fucking throw all the shit out. I don't care."

"Bullshit. You care. Whatever has crawled up your ass is making you say things you don't mean."

"Get out of my face Tobias. I swear, I'll…"

"What? Hit me?" Tobias bumped chests and huffed. "Like you could beat me."

Taylor swung.

Unluckily, his cousin was faster. The bastard punched him in the gut so hard Taylor doubled over and blew out air before falling to one knee, arms wrapped around his mid-section.

Taylor got up and tackled Tobias. They tumbled past the doorway and into the kitchen.

Before they could get up, the dogs pounced on them. Tails wagging furiously, the younger Lab, Scamp, took a hold of his jeans leg and of course the huge older Lab, Duke, decided his arm was a great toy.

"Ouch! Shit." Taylor swatted at the dog. "Stop Duke, I mean it." The Lab obviously thought it was a big game, barked and bit down on his t-shirt tugging it upward.

In the meantime, Tobias got another good punch in.

Taylor swung and missed, landing the hit to Tobias' shoulder.

"Get your damn dogs off of me." Taylor shook his foot, but Scamp hung on.

He glared at Tobias. "What the hell is wrong with you?"

His cousin gave him a droll look and whistled. The dogs immediately released their hold on Taylor and ran to the kitchen expecting a treat. Taylor sat up, but stayed on the floor. He was winded and at the moment wouldn't be averse to laying down exactly where his butt was planted.

He needed space. Had to figure out where to go and get away from everyone and everything.

"I want you, and everyone else, to get out of my face about shit. I'm…" What was he going to say? Constantly in pain? Too old for mothering?

Unfortunately, Tobias was like a dog with a bone once he got his mind set on something.

"Look dude. Whatever the hell is wrong with you, just come out with it. Stop trying to convince everyone you're okay. I know your ass is in pain constantly. I hear you moaning at night. Can't imagine what it's like for you. But you got us. You got family, and we're worried about you."

Taylor ground his teeth. "What if I told you I was too tired to give a shit about much? There is nothing more than this boring ass routine every fucking day. Wake up. Convince my busted ass to get out of bed. Go through the motions and work through the damn pain. Repeat."

"Then I'd say join the damn club. Guess what? The rest of humanity does pretty much the same thing too. It's not like most of us jump out of bed and tap dance to the shower."

"You don't get it." Taylor stood and walked toward the hallway, hoping to get to his room. But Tobias had a jump on him and blocked the way out of the kitchen.

"Nope you don't get away from this that easy." The guy crossed his arms, biceps bulging. "I think we need to go on a road trip. We'll go down and visit Janice and keep going for a bit. Maybe camp or something, get you some fresh air."

Taylor almost laughed. "Get plenty of fresh air, I work outdoors moron."

"Okay…then we can go stay at one of those resorts in Cabo San Lucas."

Taylor hitched a brow. "Should we buy matching pink trunks?"

"Don't be an ass. I'm trying to help."

"I know. Shit. I'm sorry." Giving up on escaping, Taylor pulled back a chair and sat. "Maybe I do need a vacation. The bad thing is, I'm going to be there."

"Yeah, I know. Man, you gotta take care of whatever it is that's wrong."

"Look at you, all Dr. Phil and shit."

"Fuck you. I'm better looking." Tobias yanked off his shirt and flexed.

"You're an idiot."

CHAPTER SIX

IT WAS A beautiful night and after dinner, Allison decided it would be best if she took a walk to stop from going directly to bed too early.

She felt safe outside at night there in Laurel Creek. The street which she lived on was lined with tall lampposts every fifty feet or so, which kept visibility high. After she pulled on a hoody and running shoes, Allison bounded down the stairs and out to the sidewalk.

Once outside, she took a deep breath of the cool air, loving the way her lungs expanded.

"Hi Allie!" Tori called out from across the street as her friend rushed back inside the pizzeria. How the woman worked all those hours baffled Allison. Tori seemed to be at her restaurant from late morning until it after it closed at ten o'clock at night.

Three blocks down the main road, she crossed the street to go back on the opposite side. This would be her new routine. Finish the day with a leisurely walk. Catching sight of people through windows and whoever was out either walking their dogs or on their front porch felt therapeutic.

She would definitely feel better to get fresh air and exercise instead of going straight upstairs. Most evenings ended with a meal and entire evening in front of her computer watching videos or catching up on social media. There was plenty of time for that later.

So yeah, she'd probably still end the evening with the laptop, but today it would be after getting much needed exercise.

Movement out of the corner of her eye caught her attention just as she walked back toward her shop and home. A narrow side street was darker than the sidewalk and Allison hesitated just as someone jumped out of the shadows and for a second looked toward her. The person, a man, then raced in the opposite direction and disappeared into the darkness.

Interesting.

Curious, she took a step to where the man had been, but reconsidered. She'd seen too many scary movies where people died from being nosy.

Still something bothered her, so Allison looked across the street just as the door opened and a pair of tiny dogs rushed out into the fenced-in yard. Both stopped at spotting her and began barking, their small bodies bouncing with each sound. Yap. Yap. Yap.

Deciding it was all right to investigate since she was within view of the yappers and whoever owned them, Allison took a couple of steps into the darkened area only to stop at seeing what looked to be a human hand.

It could be someone seriously hurt, or a passed out drunk the other man had robbed of whatever meager belongings. She wasn't stupid enough to go closer in case the drunk decided to jump up and kill her.

So instead, Allison yanked the phone from her pocket and called the police.

TURNED OUT, IT was worse than she imagined. The person lying on the ground was dead.

Whoever the dead man was, had been stabbed multiple times and from what she overheard had crawled to the spot in an effort to get away from his attacker.

Pausing in conversation, the officers would look to her as if she held some sort of secret.

Eric Hamilton came to where she sat on a bench outside the hardware store and patted her shoulder. In truth, Allison was not upset or frazzled. She hadn't see the person up close, so she'd been spared the sight of blood and gore.

However, understandably since she'd seen someone beside the deceased, the police insisted she remain there for the time being. Meanwhile, the forensics team from the larger nearby town was analyzing the crime scene.

It was after nine at night now and the curious folks who'd come to find out what happened had gone home. The only ones still lurking were the people across the street. Allison didn't blame them. A murder had occurred just feet from their front door.

Other than the yappers yapping, most everyone spoke in murmurs and Allison rubbed her eyes wishing she were home with a laptop and cup of tea.

"They'll need to interview you," Eric informed her.

"Again?" Allison sighed. She'd not complain. Hell at least she could complain. The man, whoever it was who'd died, did not have that privilege anymore.

"Yes, it's best to get as much information as possible while it's all still fresh in your mind."

She waited patiently until another officer came. The older man, with wisps of gray at his temples, met her gaze with understanding. Either he was well practiced at giving the impression of a well-meaning friend or he was a kind person. Either way, his presence brought a sense of trust.

He pulled out a pad and pen and lowered to sit next to her.

"You were walking in this direction," he said, motioning toward her house. "The man who you saw, would you say he was young?"

Although he asked many of the same questions Eric had asked originally, this officer had a way of bringing out more information. Finally, after what seemed like an hour later, the detective thanked her and returned to the crime scene.

"ARE YOU ALRIGHT?" Leah finally arrived. Allison had

called her best friend after realizing it would be a while before she could go home. Perhaps pretty selfish of her since Leah lived about thirty miles away, but then again, Leah would have been upset if she'd not called.

Behind Leah, Luke walked up, his bulk making everyone take notice. As they neared, the man looked from side to side, reminding her of a secret service agent, always aware of his surroundings.

After serving in several war zones, Luke who suffered from PTSD was always on alert. Truth be told, Luke actually made her feel safe and secure whenever he was around.

She looked past Luke to see two other men approaching. Tobias and Taylor walked side by side. The twins, Luke and Tobias, combined with their cousin Taylor made an impressive wide-shouldered wall of muscles.

Eric's gaze locked on Taylor. "Hey Cuz, can I talk to you for a minute?"

It was then Allison recalled Taylor had been a homicide detective and with his experience, Eric could get some help to solve the murder faster.

After a quick glance in her direction, Taylor nodded and walked a few feet away with Eric.

Whatever happened now? She yawned and looked to her friend.

Leah lowered to sit on the street bench next to her. "Eric probably called Taylor. This is horrible. Who got killed?"

Allison shrugged. "I don't know. They covered him with a blanket. I know it's a male because I overheard them say "male victim" several times."

"My goodness." Leah studied her face. "Are you okay? I bet shaken."

"Not really. I feel bad that this happened, but I didn't really see much. I thought it was someone passed out or hurt. Never thought it would be someone who was dead."

"Hopefully they'll catch who did it. Maybe you should stay with someone for a few days."

"Why would I do that?"

Leah gave her an incredulous look. "Seriously Allie, what if the guy recognizes you? You did see him after all."

"But I couldn't make out his features. He was a bit of a distance away."

"What if he thinks you got a good look at him?" Leah frowned. "I would come stay here with you, but I have to go to Billings in the morning to work for a week. Big contract."

"You can stay with us," Tobias chimed in.

"Good idea," Leah said. "You'll be safe there."

"I'm safe here. I'm sure it was some sort of misunderstanding and the guy's gone now."

"People don't get stabbed eight times over a "misunderstanding"", Taylor said, his gaze flat.

"I don't see how it has anything to do with me. I can't go anywhere." She looked to Tobias. "Thank you for the offer to stay with you, but I have a bunch of orders to fill. Too much work."

"Okay. I'll stay at your place then." Tobias crossed his arms, not giving her an option.

"You are taking the cows to Butte." Taylor gave Tobias a challenging look. "I'm not doing it."

Allison stood. "I don't need a body guard. I'm sure no one wants to stab me eight times."

Taylor frowned and moved closer taking her arm. "You saw the killer. The killer doesn't know you didn't get a good look. He probably doesn't want an eye witness who can identify him."

"Oh." Allison's heart began a drum roll type rhythm and she gasped. "I hadn't considered it that way."

"You're scaring her," Leah snapped at Taylor. "Don't be so damn mean."

"Oh goodness, you think he'll come after me?" Allison attempted to snatch her arm free while covering her mouth. She scanned the street and turned to look back toward the darkened street. Bulky jacket, tall and fast is how she'd described the assailant. Someone who could easily overpower her.

It was then she noticed Taylor still held her arm. His features were hard like granite. "I'll stay with you."

He didn't leave any room for argument.

Not that Allison would have said no. Hell she wanted all of them to stay with her now.

Several police officers remained, ensuring the crime scene was taped off and no one would traipse about and "contaminate the scene". From what Allison overheard, the crimes unit from Billings would arrive any moment now and they wanted her to remain there until they did. In case there were any more questions.

Would the night ever end?

AFTER REPEATING THE same things over and over, her brain was muddled and she'd begun to question what she saw and began giving the man who'd run a face. She let out a sigh and accepted a cup of coffee Tobias had gotten for them from her house.

Glancing across the street to her lighted shop, she wondered how in the hell she'd ever feel safe until the killer was caught. In the evenings, people could look through the windows and see inside. She often worked late tidying up to ensure everything would be ready for the next day.

The stairwell to her apartment was also visible. Although it wasn't easy to get into her apartment since she'd gotten a metal door and had a security system to rival most banks, it was still unsettling.

Taylor tapped her shoulder. "You'll be alright. No one will bother you. I doubt the guy even got a good look at you."

She'd not considered it. For a moment she thought back to when she'd seen whoever it was run. The person had looked up and directly at her before running. Above where she'd stood was a streetlight.

"He did. I stood right there under the light. I didn't quite know what was going on, so I looked toward him for a while before he looked up and saw me."

She shivered. "I think he got a good look at me."

"But you didn't." It was not a question.

"No. He was in the shadows."

It was another long two hours before they finally went across the street. Leah hugged her tightly before allowing Luke to tug her away.

Her friend looked from her to Taylor. "Please keep her safe. I mean it Taylor."

Taylor nodded. "Don't worry. You two can catch up when you get back."

When Leah sniffed and met her gaze, Allison's eyes welled up. "Go on. I'll be fine. I promise not to go anywhere without someone with me."

"Good idea." Leah left reluctantly with Luke.

Tobias lingered with them until they got inside her place. He looked around the shop as if ensuring all was safe.

The flower shop was well lit and once inside Allison was enveloped by a sense of familiarity and comfort.

"Got a flashlight?" Taylor asked and looked to Tobias. "Stay here for a moment. I want to walk around just to be sure no one's been lurking."

He glanced at Allison. "Stay down here."

When he walked out with the flashlight, Tobias lowered to a chair. "You've got the right guy here. He was a great cop."

"Sometimes I forget what he did for a living," Allison admitted.

After a few minutes, she could barely keep her eyes open.

"Go on upstairs. I'll be down here." Tobias motioned to the stairs and she didn't wait for him to repeat the request. She was not just physically but also emotionally drained.

She climbed the stairs and walked into her apartment. When she reached for the light switch, she let out a yelp when someone grabbed her and pulled her back.

On pure reflex, she elbowed the person and stomped down on his foot.

"Ow! Ouch! Damn it. I told you to wait downstairs," Taylor grumbled sidestepping another hit.

"Tobias told me to come up." Allison turned to look at him. "I thought you were outside."

"Good thing I was done. Don't you remember Tobias came up here to make coffee? The moron left the door unlocked." He pushed her behind him and glanced around the open space.

It was easy to see no one was in the main living area. Her apartment was open and bright, so he was quickly satisfied no one was about.

She went to the couch and collapsed. "Please take the bed. I sleep here on the sofa all the time. You're bigger than me and will be more comfortable in there."

His gaze went to the alarm. "What's the code?"

After she gave it to him, he set it and stood at her

kitchen counter. "Go to bed. I'll be out here."

"Nope. I insist you take the bed."

"So you can protect me when someone breaks in?"

Allison gave him a droll look. "I'm sure no one will come up here. If they do, I'll wake you up when I stuff myself under the bed."

He didn't smile. Instead he huffed and went to where she sat. Without warning, Taylor picked her up and stalked to the bedroom. Unlike every romantic fantasy she'd ever had with him, instead of lowering her to the bed and immediately joining her, he dumped her like a sack of potatoes and as she bounced almost falling to the floor, he walked out.

Twenty minutes later, she was in bed unable to sleep. She turned to the door. "Hey Taylor. You awake?"

"No."

"What do you think will happen tomorrow? Do you think they know who he is?" she called out.

Her doorway darkened and to her surprise he came and sat on the edge of the bed. His wide shoulders and broad chest strained under the plain white t-shirt he wore. From what she could make out, he still wore his jeans.

"Don't worry about it. They are questioning the deceased man's closest relatives and acquaintances right now. Tomorrow will be more of the same. This is a small community. By mid-morning, they'll have a list of possible suspects."

"Do you miss it?" Allison studied his face in the dark

and wondered if the man had any idea how handsome he was. His jawline was heavily shadowed, which suited him. Ruggedly handsome, he would make a good model for any western book.

His shrug was unconvincing. There was nothing casual about losing the ability to do the job you love. "Sometimes. Go to sleep."

Allison eyed the doorway. "You sure he won't come tonight?"

With a resigned sigh, he leaned back onto the pillows ensuring to keep one foot on the floor, which made her grin. Was he scared she'd take advantage. As enticing as the idea was, she always hated movies where people stopped for a passionate kiss or to make love, while being chased by a killer.

While distracted, people made for an easier target. Duh.

"When I was a little girl, I saw a man try to snatch another girl. The police asked me a lot of questions and I was a total wreck for a long time. My parents took turns taking me to school and if they didn't show up on time to collect me, I would freak out." Allison told him about how the girl's family had given her a huge gift for saving the day. Her screams of terror had scared the would-be kidnapper away.

At first, she wasn't sure he was snoring. But then a few moments later, it was clear she'd succeeded in putting him to sleep. Allison's lips curved into a wide grin when he shifted to his side. "Aha," she whispered.

Then ever so slowly, she slid from the bed and pulled a blanket over him. Once she was satisfied he'd not awaken, she tiptoed out.

The living room was quiet, the only light from the street lamps outside.

Her eyes barely able to remain open, she scanned the room one last time. Felt under the side cushion for her Glock and promptly fell asleep on the couch.

CHAPTER SEVEN

ALTHOUGH THE NEWS did not surprise Mindy Snyder, her heart was still shattered when a police officer came into her cafe to inform her of her brother's murder.

Only a few weeks earlier, Brian had moved in with her. He'd talked nonstop of starting a life away from drugs.

As much as she wished it to be true, a part of her never let her guard down. He'd told that same story too many times.

By his jumpy demeanor and the constant refusal to go anywhere, she suspected he was in some sort of trouble. It had to be either the law or some drug dealer after money he owed.

More than once she'd asked if he needed money to pay someone off or if he'd had caused someone so much harm, they'd come after him.

Every single time Brian would react badly. He was defensive and refused to talk about it. Her brother had done something terrible or terribly wrong to the point someone wanted him dead.

Whoever it was that killed her brother had been enraged. The police suspected the killer knew Brian. The killer had been so angry at something, they'd stabbed him enough times to ensure he was truly dead.

Her tissue fell apart when she dabbed at the constant flow of tears. The police officer, Eric Hamilton, pulled a handkerchief out of his back pocket and handed it to her.

For a moment she looked up and met his gaze. No one carried handkerchiefs anymore that she knew of. "Thank you."

She sniffed loudly into the cloth wishing everyone in the shop to disappear. It was closed for business, however her employee was busy making coffee and toasting bagels and such for the law enforcement officers who'd come to town for the investigation.

Two detectives from Billings joined Eric and his partner Jacob Myers. There were a few other people seated at tables by the windows whom she assumed were crime scene investigators. None of them spoke to her, leaving the detectives to do the questioning.

"I'm sorry, we need to find out as much as we can about Brian and what he was doing since arriving here," a detective said, his eyes moving from her face to the handkerchief she wrapped and unwrapped around her finger.

"I understand," Mindy replied. And although she

did, at the same time she was frustrated at herself for not having asked Brian more questions.

She should have insisted he tell her the truth about what happened. Under the guise of not wanting to cause him more stress, she'd probably made matters worse.

"He was hiding something or from someone. Although he'd been living with me for almost three months, I can probably count on one hand the times he left the house."

The detective exchanged looks with Eric who lowered to sit next to her. "What did he do all day?"

"Cleaned, fixed things. My house has never been so perfect. Every item that needed the slightest fixing, he took care of. Most days he insisted on cooking and such. Of course he'd give me a list and ask me to pick up items at the grocery store."

This time the detective spoke. "Did you not find it odd that he never left the house? What reasons did he give you for not going out?"

"Of course I found it odd. The only outdoors place he went was in the back yard. He'd mow the lawn and such. Sometimes, he'd sit on my back-porch swing for hours, just thinking."

"And the reason he gave you?" Eric prodded.

Mindy wanted to scream with frustration. Her only brother was dead and they wanted her to relive every single conversation she'd had with him.

"I knew he was detoxing from drug use. Meth. Said it was embarrassing to go out in public because he shook so much. Especially when he was tired or nervous."

Eric Hamilton's hazel gaze met hers. "Did he? Did he shake a lot?"

Now that she considered it, she rarely noticed it. Every once in a while, when they ate, his hand would shake a bit. "Sometimes. It was barely noticeable. I mentioned it to him. Told him he seemed steady enough to me. But he'd ignore my comments."

She slid to the edge of the seat. Her leg touched Eric's and for a moment it jolted her thoughts away from what she was about to say. Clearing her throat, she moved to the side a bit so they'd not touch.

"Look, I knew something was off. I suspected he either owed someone money or had stolen drugs. He was my only brother and we were close. I know...knew him well. He trusted me."

The detective held out a hand to stop Eric from saying something. "Is that why he came here? To your house instead of other family members?"

"My father is remarried and lives in Seattle. Mom and Brian had a huge falling out because of his drug use. He'd not go there."

Eric studied her for a long moment until she wondered what he'd been on the brink of asking.

She turned to him. "Why do you think someone killed my brother?"

He looked to the detective before meeting her gaze again. How had she not noticed the striking color of his eyes? The palest green with golden specks, they were a stark contrast to his olive toned complexion.

Without expression, he spoke, "I think it was personal. Whoever killed your brother knew him and was angry at something that had transpired between them. It could be he owed the person money, but I suspect it went deeper than that."

"Oh." Mindy couldn't think of anything Brian ever said that indicated someone was angry with him. Then again, he'd been especially quiet the last few weeks.

"When can I see about getting my brother's body and prepare for his funeral?"

The detective motioned to a woman who'd introduced herself as a medical examiner earlier. The woman gave her an understanding look. "Unfortunately, it could be at least a week. With this being a murder investigation, we need to examine him and ensure every injury is documented. Also search for any evidence that could be found."

Mindy's phone chimed and she closed her eyes. It was time to call her parents and inform them of what happened. She'd avoided it until she'd be able to give them more answers. Both would be there within hours, demanding answers and probably ask her the same questions the police had.

CHAPTER EIGHT

T AYLOR HADN'T SLEPT so well in a long time. The bed was so comfortable that for the first time in a long time, he was not in a hurry to get up.

His hip even seemed less painful than most mornings as the softness enveloped him lulling him to sleep deeper.

Suddenly remembering he'd not gone to sleep in his own bed, Taylor's eyes flew open. "What in the living hell?"

The softness of white on white and modern furnishings combined with some sort of soothing music was not a bad way to wake up. However on this day it was embarrassing. He was there to guard Allison, not to be put to bed like a pansy-ass and sleep in as if he was on some sort of spa vacation.

The smell of coffee tickled his nose and he rolled over and pressed his face into the pillow. It smelled of her. A soft flowery scent that suited Allison perfectly.

At this point it made no sense to hurry to get up. Hell, he actually considered procrastinating until she went downstairs to work. But that probably wasn't for a couple hours from then. He looked at his wrist. Watch was gone.

Along with his wallet and cell phone, it was on the bedside table next to a vase of flowers. Well wasn't he just the most watchful guard on the planet?

He checked, and yeah he still had pants on, but they'd been unbuttoned to allow him to be more comfortable. Either he'd been tired as hell, or Allison was magical.

Hating to give up his comfortable spot, he sat up and stretched. His hip barely protested. The real test would be standing up. The fucker always made him want to cut off his leg most mornings.

Sure enough, the sharp pain shot through his hip. However, it wasn't bad enough to consider finding the closest sharp saw.

He didn't bother with his watch and instead left the room and walked into Allison's main living area. It had been shocking to walk into her apartment the night before.

The entire top floor of her grandmother's house was transformed into a modern space, like nothing he'd ever seen before. The walls were a soft gray, the furniture all in muted tones of either gray or white. Although at the tall kitchen counter there were three tall bright red stools, and matching crimson pillows on the white leather couches, the rest of the space lacked much color.

While he would have thought it would be sterile, it

was more peaceful than anything else.

From her kitchen, a person could see past the living room to huge floor to ceiling windows framing the view of the mountains.

"Good morning." She stood in the kitchen wearing colorful leggings and an oversized long-sleeved gray top. Her curls hung freely, landing softly on her shoulders.

"Sorry about falling asleep on your bed." He brushed a hand through his hair. "You all right?"

"I would say I'm great, but that would be a lie," she replied motioning for him to get coffee. "I slept well enough, but woke up early to rehash what happened last night."

He understood. Sometimes victims or witnesses would call him early in the mornings to ask questions after having settled down and the reality of what happened sunk in.

The coffee maker was a bright red and he wondered if it was her favorite color. "Your place is very different from what I expected."

With a soft smile, she looked around with an assessing eye. "When I moved here and had to remodel, I decided to go for it. I wanted a place that I could feel relaxed and at home without fuss. It cost me a good amount, but it's totally worth it. I did not compromise on anything."

It was obvious from the light fixtures to the modern tile he'd noticed in the bathroom, she did not spare expense.

"Your bed, what kind of mattress is that?" He planned to buy one immediately.

She tapped her fingers on the side of the cup in thought. "I'll get you the info. It's one of those memory foam mattresses. It's pricey, but well worth it. You should get one, it helps with bad hips and such." Her gaze moved to his mid-section and he turned sideways to keep from her noticing the affect it had.

Finally, she went to the living room. He followed her movements. Allison wasn't slender, more what he'd call medium build, but with a definite softness that brought attention to her rounded bottom and long graceful legs. He was more than attracted to her. If it wasn't for all his baggage, there was little that would have stopped him from going after her.

This game of playing bodyguard was a dangerous one. If he wasn't careful it could turn complicated quick.

She looked to him, the sunlight behind her framing her beauty perfectly. "The only thing I have for breakfast is oatmeal and maybe a couple of bagels. It doesn't look like Mindy's place is open this morning. Very strange."

He went to the kitchen window and sure enough the café was closed. Not only that, but Eric's truck was parked in front along with several other cars. Either the cops had taken over the only breakfast place in town to eat, or the murder from the night before had something to do with the owner. He guessed the second option.

He went to the bedroom and called Eric, who answered on the second ring. "Hey Cuz. Where you at?"

Within moments he knew the reason for the café being closed. Allison watched him while toasting bagels. Her eyes tracked his every movement.

"What happened?" she asked as soon as he ended the call.

"Brian, the owner's brother is who was killed."

Brows moving together, her eyes moved side to side. "Oh no. I didn't know Mindy had a brother here."

"Seems he was loner. Rarely went anywhere since moving here."

She placed a toasted bagel before him and he climbed onto the stool to eat. Once his coffee was refilled, he decided it was best to discuss the logistics of the next couple days.

"What time do you have to be here to open the shop?"

"Nine, I open at ten." She bit from her bagel and narrowed her eyes. "Why?"

"I have to help out at the ranch. So maybe we can go there after you close shop. I can work til evening, we'll stay there overnight, come here early and you can open your shop."

"Why don't you stay here, go to the ranch once I am downstairs and come back for the evening?"

"Because you'll be alone most of the day."

"It's daylight. There are windows on two sides. I can keep the door locked and open only when customers walk up."

"How will you tell the difference between a customer

and a killer? I don't think the person will be holding a knife up to identify him or herself."

Allison rolled her eyes, but he knew she considered his question by the way her teeth sunk into her bottom lip. "Crud."

"Oh, I know," she said holding up a finger. "I can put up a sign that says "surveillance camera in use"." A slow smile curved her lips and he almost smiled with her.

"That won't work." He looked past her to the digital time display on her microwave. "Shouldn't you be getting dressed?"

She leaned across the counter and grinned at him. "Wanna guard me while I do?"

Yes, he really did.

ALLISON HAD TO admit, it was a fun and enticing game to be so close to Taylor, but still not quite within reach. The way he tracked her every move had nothing to do with him guarding her safety.

Both knew damn well that if he continued to stay at her place, they'd end up sharing the bed. Tobias' presence at the ranch would be a deterrent, but not exactly a guarantee they'd not sleep together. It would happen sooner or later, but being at her apartment made it a surety.

Guilty that she thought more about her attraction to Taylor that morning than what had transpired the night before, Allison said a quick prayer for Mindy and her brother.

Although she didn't know Mindy well, she'd ensure to call or send flowers that day. No one should lose a family member in such a brutal way.

Finally dressed, she walked out to find Taylor on the phone. He paced like a caged lion, back and forth, head down, his free hand on his hip.

"Yeah, I know."

He didn't stop walking.

"All right. Okay. Next week."

He stopped pacing, turning to face the windows. His broad shoulders lifted and lowered.

"Monday. I promise. You too."

When he turned, Taylor looked her over. "Ready for the day?"

She nodded. "I insist you go take care of whatever needs to be done at the ranch. I'll be okay. Just come back some time tonight. We can hunker down after dinner."

An hour later she repeated the statement. Ignoring her, Taylor went to the door and looked out. "It's quiet today."

"It usually is."

Several customers had come and gone. Most commenting on the murder and discussing what they thought had happened and why. Thankfully none knew she was a witness.

A couple walked in, after greeting Taylor, the woman went about shopping while the man sat at the table and accepted a cup of coffee.

Seeming satisfied the steady flow of customers would be a good deterrent for anyone to harm her, Taylor finally left.

As much as she enjoyed having him around, it was hard to concentrate with him there. Once the day was over, she'd ensure to discuss a better alternative to him being her bodyguard.

There was the idea of closing the shop for a few days, but then she'd still be there alone upstairs, which would be boring and drive her crazy.

Staying at the Hamilton ranch was not an option. She'd go bonkers there too. Perhaps she could return to Billings and spend time there. Then again, she'd scheduled deliveries for a wedding the following week, she had arrangements and bouquets to make.

The murder was affecting her life in too many ways.

CHAPTER NINE

S HE KNEW WHEN Taylor walked into the shop. It was
as if the air suddenly stilled and electrical currents
charged the air. Allison tried her best not to allow the
elderly woman to see how he affected her. It was useless
as the woman looked to Taylor then to Allison and
smiled in a knowing way.

"I think your friend will love this arrangement. Let
me ring up the gift for you as well." Allison moved to
stand behind her small counter and tapped the screen.

"Have an enjoyable evening." The woman tapped
Taylor's arm. "Tell your aunt hello for me. I haven't seen
her in ages."

"Yes ma'am," Taylor said, holding the door open for
the woman.

The room dimmed when she turned off the floral
display lights and then the overhead lights, leaving the
room in shadows.

"Did you eat dinner yet?" she asked Taylor, who'd
moved to stand by the stairs. "I've got minestrone soup

in the crockpot and am going to make grilled cheese to go with it."

He nodded, which told her nothing and silently followed her up the stairs. The silence made her even more aware of his presence. What was it with the damn silent treatment today? Was he pissed about having to come there?

Once inside her apartment, the aroma of soup and the low hum of music greeted them. She always left the music station playing on the television. The soft sounds of jazz made her place less silent at the end of the day.

"Are you in a bad mood?" Allison asked as he walked to the windows and looked up and down the street, scanning it methodically. Both hands on his slender hips showcased the wide expanse of his back and broad shoulders. His ass was not bad either.

"They've got a lead. Think it's a guy from Billings. If so, he's probably back there now. Eric is there now and hopefully he'll call shortly and let us know they've got him."

So it meant it was probably his last night there. Allison pulled out a skillet and reached for a loaf of bread she'd bought at the Farmer's Market just two days prior.

"I hope they do catch him. I'd feel better not imposing so much on you with all this."

Taylor neared, his gaze intent. "It's not an imposition at all. I'm glad to be of help. If anything, it's added something interesting to my boring days."

"You don't have boring days. All that work out there

at the ranch. I know you're probably falling behind…"

His kiss took her by surprise. So much so, the loaf of bread landed on the floor next to her foot. The previous hunger for food turned to starvation to have Taylor instead.

While he ravaged her mouth, his hands slid down her sides to cup her butt and pull her against his hardness. And damn was he hard.

"Fuck," he muttered against her lips before once again covering her mouth and pushing his tongue deep.

It was like no other kiss before, this time the request was real and strong. So much transpired in the kiss, the way he moaned and pulled her against his body made her legs wobble and her knees weaken.

"I want you Allison." He pressed a kiss just below her ear. This time she couldn't keep silent, a soft sound came from her lips.

"Yes," she said, finally able to formulate words.

Before she could say or do anything else, Taylor continued to kiss her while walking her backwards to the bedroom. He wasn't wasting time. Any thought would mean one or both could come to the realization of what a huge mistake they were about to make.

Their mouths fused, they continued the savage kiss while undressing. Her dress was first to go leaving her in just bra and panties.

His shoes were followed by hers. Breaking the kiss, he yanked his t-shirt off and Allison lost her breath. He was perfectly built.

Allison ran her hands over his chest, her eyes locked to his as he unfastened her bra.

Palms over her breasts, he rubbed in circular motions and Allison head to fell back allowing the wonderful sensations free rein.

His mouth followed, trailing kisses from her breast-bone down to take her left nipple into his mouth. He sucked it in hard and she moaned as tingles shot straight down her stomach to between her legs.

The man knew what he was doing. His hand slid under the elastic of her skimpy panties to between her legs and he cupped her sex.

"Ah." She gulped in air and grabbed his shoulders. "Oh."

When he began massaging the juncture between her legs while his mouth moved to the right breast, Allison about lost it.

The tresses of his hair were soft between her fingers as Allison held him in place at her breast needing more of the wicked things his tongue was doing.

His thumb circled her clit and she fell to pieces. Thankfully his mouth covered hers just as she cried out. No need to alarm anyone who could possibly overhear. Although it was doubtful anyone could past the thick walls and double-paned windows.

Taylor held her against him as the last of the waves of her climax worked through.

They moved to stand beside the bed and he lowered Allison's panties down her legs. On wobbly legs, she stood still allowing him to take her in fully. Lips curved, his darkened gaze raked over her inch by inch. It was as if he touched every place his eyes landed, heat surfacing each spot.

Breathing became a struggle when he continued his perusal, sending Allison to heights of desire she'd never felt before.

Finally Taylor met her gaze.

What seemed like a flicker of uncertainty in his expression turned to challenge when he removed his box-briefs. It was then she noticed the scarring.

Just above the waistband of his briefs on the left side was a ragged scar that ran down to his upper thigh. His thigh was misshapen. Ugly scars pulled at the skin, making the area dip in. If anything, the marks made him sexier and even more desirable. Allison bit her bottom lip and focused for a moment longer trailing upwards past his washboard abs to his well-formed chest. He was more than an eyeful that was for sure.

Although she wanted to take him all in, memorize every bit of the masculinity before her, it was hard to concentrate when his thick erection demanded all the attention.

"Wow."

When she met his gaze, he rolled his eyes playfully. "Is that all women think about?"

Allison sucked in her bottom lip and smiled. "I don't know of any woman that would be able to ignore you. Come here." She crooked her finger at him and Taylor's eyebrows rose.

She couldn't help the sharp intake of breath, sounding more like a gasp when he came closer. Somehow she had to memorize every instant, commit to memory this wonderful night.

Finally, Taylor Hamilton would be hers.

DAMN IF HE didn't almost come just by looking at Allison. The soft lighting filtering in from the living room was enough to let him to see her clearly.

From her long legs to her rounded hips, she was perfection. Unlike women he'd been with before, she was assured enough to allow him to take his time to admire her body.

He hated it when women focused too much on the imperfections and attempted to hide themselves. Not Allison.

She was plush, with a soft mound for a stomach and a hint of a roll above her waist. That place in particular, just above her waist made his mouth water and he couldn't wait to lick and nip at the soft skin.

When she crooked her finger inviting him to join her in bed, she didn't have to repeat herself.

Taking her with him, they tumbled onto the bed and he instantly wanted to be inside of her.

When she giggled, he was relieved. He was a damn idiot. Had to take things slower. What he wanted more than anything at the moment was to dive into her and fuck her until he came. But that would happen soon enough. For now, he'd follow her lead.

"I want you Taylor. Can't make up my mind if I want to enjoy touching and kissing, take our time or to demand you fuck me hard and fast."

He took the decision away from her. "We can do both."

He covered her mouth while settling between her thighs, the plushness almost enough to make him senseless. Taking his dick in hand, he maneuvered to her center and thrust in.

"Ah!" both said in unison, stilling for a moment. She was hot, wet and tight. Taylor wasn't sure he could move an inch without losing control.

Good thing his body took over independently. He pulled out and dove back into her, the movement steady while he could keep it. Each time however sent him farther into what was all Allison. The sounds she made combined with the silky skin and softness of her body made his entire world spin.

This would not be a give and take. No way in hell.

He took all and thankfully so did Allison. She cried out, her nails digging into his ass until his entire body shook.

Only a couple thrusts more and he was unable to stop the climax. He came so hard his eyes crossed and toes curled.

When he collapsed on top of her, Allison began twirling her tongue just below his ear and damn if his cock didn't stir.

Yeah, round two would be slow and steady.

CHAPTER TEN

TAYLOR SLEPT LIKE he made love. With reckless abandon.

Currently, he was sprawled across her bed. One arm above his head, the other across his midsection, he'd kicked off most of the blankets and was only covered across the hips with the sheet.

With every breath his chest expanded, calling to her to touch and feel the wide expanse. She gave in and ran her hand over the heated skin, enjoying the valleys and hills of the muscles down his stomach. Although he shifted, Taylor didn't wake. Instead, he turned his face away and continued sleeping.

Her lips curved as she kissed the dip between his pecs and trailed her tongue down past his flat stomach. Then taking his sex in hand, she licked from the base to the tip, hesitating when his breathing hitched.

After twirling her tongue around the tip, his hips jutted upward, a clear signal to proceed. She opened wide to allow the thickness of him to push past her lips.

Allison made sure to prolong the moment until he lost control and yanked her over atop him and drove into her body.

AFTER ANOTHER BOUT of lovemaking, Taylor excused himself to shower and Allison pulled an oversized t-shirt over leggings and went to the kitchen. She pondered what would happen next. Of course he'd try to let her down gently.

Would it be the "I've got too much going on right now", or the "This was a one-time thing"?

She stirred creamer into her coffee and watched as the color lightened. It would be the latter. He'd be nice about it, but it would still be awkward.

A breeze blew in through the open kitchen window chilling the room and she took in a deep breath. These few moments before he came out of her bedroom were perfect. To pretend it was the start of a relationship and that he would admit to wanting to spend more time with her. Yes it was silly, but she did just that.

Just then across the street a man stopped and looked up at her window. For a moment or two they locked gazes. He was young, perhaps thirty and wore a thick blue jacket. Chills traveled up her spine. Could it be the killer?

Was he the man on the dark street two days ago? She looked behind to see if Taylor was there and considered reaching for her phone, but it was on the coffee table.

When she looked back the man was gone. It couldn't be him. The killer would be long gone by now. It was her imagination at work. Of course, that was it.

"Is something wrong?"

Allison jerked around, coffee sloshing out of her cup. She put it down and wiped the counter with a dishtowel.

"No...I don't think so."

When he neared, she could see what made him a good detective. He immediately looked out the window and then met her gaze. "What happened?"

"How did you know I was nervous?"

"I saw you look out the window searching, your right hand across your chest."

Now she felt even more ill at ease. Taylor had been watching her and she'd not noticed.

She let out a long sigh. "I'm sure it's my imagination. I looked out and there was a man standing there." She pointed to a street sign.

"He was looking up here at my window. And then when I looked again, he was gone."

Taylor came up beside her and put his arm around her shoulders. The gesture made Allison want to cry. "Was there something about him that was familiar?"

"I don't know. I can't say. It was strange. We kinda stared at each other for a moment. He didn't smile or wave or nothing. Is that weird? Am I being stupid? Please tell me."

"No not at all. It's natural to be suspicious right now. He could have just been admiring you and got caught."

She wanted to believe him. However, the man seemed to be mad when she looked at him. Again, probably her overactive brain even less affective since the night before.

Allison hugged him and then moved back. "You should go on to work. I'll be fine. Don't worry about coming over. I'm closed today and tomorrow, so I'll go visit my friend in Billings and stay there until the day after tomorrow. Hopefully this will all be over by then."

"A friend?" His brow crinkled.

"Yes. Hilda. She took over my flower shop there when I moved here. I'll contact her and I'm sure she won't mind me spending a couple days there."

"Not a good idea. I don't know that I like the idea of you driving alone out of town." He motioned to the coffeepot and Allison moved back so he could pour.

He turned and studied her for a moment. "Come on, let's have breakfast. I want to go to the café and make sure the owner is all right. Looks like it's open."

Allison laughed. "Umm, I don't have any make up on. I don't want to know what my hair looks like right now and look at my outfit."

When he took her in, Allison was astounded when Taylor seemed pleased with what he saw. "You look perfect to me."

"After breakfast, we're getting your eyes checked." She rushed to the bathroom and splashed water on her face. Allison then finger combed her hair up into a messy loose bun. When she swiped on lip-gloss Taylor leaned in from the doorway. "Ready?"

She nodded and allowed him to lead her out. While she locked the door, Taylor pressed a kiss to her neck. "Thanks for the wake up."

The warmth of his breath could not compete with the heat that crept up from that spot and now her face was probably beet red.

That certainly completed her 'awkward, no make up obviously just rolled out of bed look'.

CHAPTER ELEVEN

MINDY LET OUT a breath as Taylor and Allison walked in. It was the second time she'd seen them together. They seemed to be getting along better than the first time, by the lingering of his hand on her back and the way she smiled at him. As if a secret passed between them.

New relationships were always so fresh and exciting. Although she'd not dated in a couple of years, it made her want to smile despite the current circumstances.

"Good morning," Allison greeted her. "How are you feeling?"

In truth, she felt guilty. Either her brother's death had not sunk in, or the fact her parents had taken over her house, filling it with hilarious, continuous bickering and barking of dogs helped. Although she was sure her parents didn't understand her sense of humor from hearing them argue over everything.

Both had brought a dog. The dogs didn't get along any better than they did. Although she'd planned to close the café for the week, she'd been glad to get out of the house and escape.

"I'm good. My parents are here…" Mindy left the sentence hanging, not sure what to add.

Both placed their orders and her employee began to make the coffee and bagels.

"I'm so sorry for your loss Mindy," Allison said. "I didn't know your brother was living here."

Mindy nodded. "Nobody really knew, he was pretty much a recluse. Had a lot of issues."

She accepted a hug from Allison.

Taylor hung back, his gaze moving from her face to behind her to the coffee machine. All the Hamilton's were very handsome. However, she found Taylor to be distinct. Just as attractive as the twins, he stood out however with a deep cleft in his chin.

Muscular like Tobias and Luke, his presence filled a room. And with a background in law enforcement like Eric Hamilton, he gave the sense of knowing more than was obvious.

He was normally easy-going and always friendly when she'd seen him around town. But there was a standoffish air about him at the same time.

"Notice any new people come in for coffee in the last couple days?" he asked in a flat voice.

Her mind immediately went back to the man she'd seen that morning, maybe twenty minutes earlier. He'd stood outside the café peering in, his expression somber.

"No. Other than the usuals, just a family that was

passing through on their way to Cartersville."

"See a guy in a blue jacket, perhaps mid thirties?" he prompted.

Her heart skipped a bit. "Yes. He stood outside and looked in. But he didn't come inside."

"Seen him before?"

She motioned for her employee to serve a woman who'd walked in. Meanwhile, Mindy carried their coffee and bagels on a tray to a table.

"No never. Didn't look familiar. Should I be concerned?"

Taylor's brows lowered. "Probably not. Just be sure to keep someone with you when you're here."

Although it was good that he didn't try to bullshit her, his lack of assurance didn't help her feel better. "Okay. I'm rarely alone here in the café. My parents are coming before closing so we can go out to dinner."

"Good." He looked toward the booth. "Should you need anything, give me a call. Eric will be back from Billings later today. I'll make sure he updates you."

Mindy scanned the café, the familiarity of it setting her mind at ease. If Eric didn't call or stop there by nightfall, she'd call him. Hopefully they'd caught the man who'd killed Brian. She squeezed her eyes shut.

Maybe it was too soon for her to be there, but other than sitting at home overcome by sadness, she'd had to get out and do something normal.

TAYLOR SETTLED ACROSS from Allison. He was glad she'd not put makeup on or did whatever women do to fix up. Natural and dressed in the clothes she'd pulled on after making love made him want to pound his chest and let everyone know she'd been his that morning.

Yeah, pretty primitive and embarrassingly teenage emotions, but he'd enjoy it for the moment. Hell, it'd been a long time since he'd felt so much excitement over a woman.

The reality of what he'd been putting off would settle in soon. For now, having been woken up with a beautiful woman sucking him off made him want to drag her back to her place and do a repeat.

Even his hip had barely bothered him that morning. He'd massaged it in the shower under the hot streams of water to keep from limping like he did most mornings. The combination of the amazing mattress and the shower had done wonders.

He'd not taken the painkillers since the day before. Well what do you know?

"What are you so deep in thought about?" Allison's question brought him back to reality.

A slight blush across her cheeks made him smile. "Sorry. I was staring, wasn't I?"

"A little." Her lips curved and she sipped the coffee. "What are you doing today?"

He shrugged. "Same as usual. Working at the ranch and watching you."

"I'm going to Billings today."

"No, you're not."

She blinked, her brows lifting. "Excuse me?"

"I'm not comfortable with you leaving knowing some guy's lurking around. He could follow you."

For a moment, she hesitated and then released a huff. "He's not a super hero. How's he going to know I'm going anywhere? I'm going to Billings," she repeated.

"Fine. I'll take you."

"No you won't. You don't have to do that."

"It's best if I take you."

She looked toward the counter. "I forgot to ask her when the funeral is."

"Next week."

Mindy caught her eye and rounded the counter. "My parents want to meet with you about flowers. Do you have time today or tomorrow?"

Allison nodded, noting Taylor's smug lift of his lips. "Yes of course. Either day works."

She let out a sigh when Mindy went back greeting a woman who walked in and hugged her. "I guess that means I'm staying in town."

"Good idea."

When Allison laughed, the husky sound made him chuckle.

"You did not win this argument." She lifted a brow in challenge. "I don't want to be a burden. How about if I ask Tori if I can stay at her place tonight so you can get more work done?"

"How about you come stay at the ranch for the next

two nights?"

"With you? Oh no. I'm not sure I want to do that."

He gave her a droll look although he wondered what she meant by "that". "We have a spare room. Luke's old bedroom."

"I don't know." She bit her lip. "I wish Leah was back."

CHAPTER TWELVE

MINDY'S HEART SKIPPED a beat when Eric Hamilton walked through the front door.

Hopefully he'd bring good news. It was time for them to put Bryan to rest and her family to move on. As if in some sort of alternate reality, she and her parents went through the motions of every day life in a fog. Like when her grandmother died, the aftermath of death was always such a hard thing. With her brother being so young and his death a murder, it was even harder to grasp and fathom that he was gone so suddenly.

The expression on Eric's face gave little indication of what he was about to say. His steely gaze moved from the display of pastries to her face. "Hello Mindy."

Two simple words and yet in that moment once again her breath hitched at his deep voice saying it.

"Any news?" The customers in the shop were obviously aware of what had happened. Little could be kept secret in Laurel Creek. Heads turned following Eric's trail to where she stood.

He moved closer and spoke in a soft voice. It was comical when two ladies seated at a nearby table leaned forward, their eyes locked on Eric.

"We have a suspect. There is a warrant out. Just waiting. I came back here in case he returns for whatever reason."

She thought back to the man she'd seen earlier and her skin crawled. "What does he look like?"

Eric took her by the arm and guided her to a small storage room away from the prying eyes and ears. Once inside the tight space, the intimacy of the closed quarters made her hypersensitive.

"Did you see someone?" His gaze bore into hers.

"I think so. No one I knew. But there was a man in a blue jacket. He stood outside for a long while this morning. He gave me a strange feeling. I called my parents and told them to lock the doors and stay inside." She sighed. "Probably just me being paranoid."

"No, it's understandable and actually a good idea until the guy's caught."

It was hard to look him in the face. He was so much taller than her and although slightly slimmer than the other Hamiltons, he was not a small guy. Although he'd yet to release her arm, she wasn't about to ask him to. It was reassuring; the touch and the strength emanating from him.

Brows drawn together, he was quiet as she described the man she'd seen. Young, about thirty, with dark brown hair and glasses. The fairly nondescript guy would normally never stand out. But with it being so soon after the murder, everyone who was unfamiliar got her attention.

"Sounds like a reporter who was nosing around. If he comes in here and starts asking questions, let me know."

ALLISON JOGGED DOWN the stairs and through the shop to answer the door. The constant bell ringing although the sign on the window was turned off was surprising. One of the downsides of living above your business was the locals knew you were there.

The wife of a prominent rancher walked in along with her air of entitlement.

If only Allison would have ignored the bell.

"How can I help you today? I'm currently closed."

The woman lifted a brow. "Oh, I didn't notice. The lights were on."

Allison looked up to the darkened lights and waited.

"I need flowers for an impromptu afternoon get-together. I require two large centerpieces, an arrangement for the bathroom and another two for my sitting room. Can you manage that while I go over to pick up some food?"

She placed both hands across her ample bosom following up with a dramatic sigh. "Everyone thinks it's so easy to host these things. With only a day's notice."

Allison wouldn't know but she nodded sympathetically. "When do you need this by?"

The woman glanced at her diamond-studded watch. "Two hours? Is that enough time?

"Not really." Allison scanned her limited selection of flowers. "A new shipment doesn't come in until Monday. If you don't mind them being simple, I may be able to come up with the arrangements for you."

"Fine." The woman's aggravated sigh made Allison fight hard not to roll her eyes. "I'll be back at 4." She left without giving any information. No name, phone number or anything. Obviously everyone was supposed to know who she was.

As soon as the woman left, her cell dinged. It was a text from Taylor.

Have to go out of town.
Texted Eric. He's back.
Let me know if you have a
Place to stay tonight.
You can still come here.

She read the text several times. Actually Taylor leaving town worked out well. She'd have time to make the arrangements, ensure the place was locked up tight and stay there.

Daylight always gave people courage. The shadows and night sounds would strip it away, of that she had no doubts.

Through the window, the patrol car was parked in front of the café. Allison grabbed her sweatshirt from the back of a chair, picked up her keys and headed out.

The bell over the café door dinged and every eye turned to her. Two women were at one table sipping coffee. At another table, a couple chatted over sandwiches and drinks.

There was no one behind the counter. One of the women looked to her. "They are in the back office. Mindy and the policeman."

It was best to wait. Allison sat at the closest table.

When Eric walked out, Allison asked about what Taylor had texted.

Eric had not seen Taylor's text and quickly scanned it after Allison told him.

While reading, he motioned her outside. "Too many perked ears in there," he said with a smile. They walked back to her shop together.

Once inside, he placed his cell back into his front shirt pocket. "Look, I don't want you staying here alone. Although we have a suspect, he's still out there. Can you stay somewhere?"

It would be an inconvenience, but she nodded. "Yes." Allison told him about the guy she'd seen from her window.

Eric seemed sure the suspect was in Billings and the guy she and Mindy had seen was a reporter. Once he left, she began to quickly put the arrangements together for the woman. Glad for the work as it was a great distractor.

TORI'S LAUGHTER RANG out as Allison talked about the encounter with the snooty woman who'd returned for the centerpieces.

"I suppose they will have to do," the woman had stated and made a production of pulling twenty-five dollars from her Louis Vuitton wallet. "For your effort."

"What do you plan to do with all that cash?" Tori asked. "Don't spend it all in one place."

"I got this bottle of wine and we're going to order takeout. How about that?"

Tori shook her head. "No pizza please."

Just a few blocks from the flower shop, Tori lived in a cute one-story cottage. Every time Allison drove or walked by, it reminded her of a fairytale house.

She looked around the space. Tori's taste for décor was Allison's absolute opposite. Where Allison preferred clean lines, Tori's home was more on the eclectic side. The colorful throw pillows on a bright red couch and modern art on the walls matched Tori's bubbly personality.

The petite woman had worn her hair waist length in high school. Now her hair was a flattering pixie cut. Dangling earrings shimmered from her ears as she turned to face where Allison sat.

"You know, it's so nice to spend time with you now. Remember how we always used to hang out at each other's houses?"

"Until you started dating Tobias," Allison quipped. "Then it was all googly eyes and kissy-kissy faces."

Tori sighed. "Those days things were so simple." Her bright eyes snapped to Allison. "Speaking of the Hamiltons, what's up with you and Taylor? You seemed pretty engrossed in each other the other night."

"Yeah, it's kinda strange. I'm not sure what's going on between us. We had sex. It was amazing." Allison giggled. "I can't believe it. Remember how I used to obsess over him?"

"Do I?" Tori laughed. "You would flush and start sweating any time he came around. You and him never got together back then?"

"No," Allison exclaimed. "I was too tongue-tied to do more than stare at him and try to breathe. And then I dated Jake for the last two years of high school."

"So, it was amazing huh?" Tori sipped her wine. "I miss amazing sex."

"No one in your life then either huh?"

"Nope. I haven't dated in a couple of years. With the restaurant, I barely have time to breathe. Sometimes I think I should sell it. I want to do something else. I just wish I knew what."

They sat in companionable silence. Both looked at the television screen, but not really watching the movie.

"What happened between you and Tobias? You never said why you broke off the engagement." The wine gave Allison the boldness to ask. She'd already moved to Billings when she learned from Leah that Tori and Tobias had cancelled their wedding.

Tori looked down into her wine. "You know, it

seems so childish now. Instead of supporting him, giving him encouragement while he fought overseas, I wrote him a Dear John letter."

"Oh goodness. Why did you do that?"

"I was terrified for him. I didn't want to continuously freak out every time I heard something in the news. I hated every minute of it. I broke it off because I didn't want to be his girlfriend if he died over there. The stupid thing was, after we broke up, I hated not knowing. So I was always glued to the news sites even more."

"You were eighteen Tori. Give yourself a break. War is a hard thing for a teenager to handle."

Tori shook her head. "Maybe. But he was barely past his teens himself and was over there fighting. He put his life on the line and I was so horrible to him. If something had happened to him, I would have never forgiven myself."

"Sounds to me like you haven't forgiven yourself now."

"Maybe." Tori got up and got the wine bottle. After refilling Allison's, she topped her own off. "You know all we do is fight now. Every time I see him. He knows exactly what to say or do to piss me off."

"Where there's smoke..." Allison wiggled her eyebrows. When Tori glared, she picked up her cell phone. "Does Chinese sound good?"

CHAPTER THIRTEEN

I T HAD BEEN a long time since Taylor had driven down the familiar streets in Caspar, Wyoming. His truck ambled at a low speed as he scanned the neighborhood street where he and his family had lived.

The cool air that wafted through the cracked windows smelled of snow and he wondered how long before the first flake fell. Although it was probably too early for a snow flurry, for some reason he wished for it.

Immediately a picture of a young boy crouched down beside him formed. They'd hid behind a short wall waiting for his wife and daughter to come out.

Once they got to the car, they'd started throwing from the pile of white ammunition they'd made. It had been hilarious to watch Janice run in circles screaming while his daughter giggled.

There had been shrieks and promises of retaliation as both had dashed back inside.

Janice had rushed back to the house and screamed at them. "I'm locking the door. You're both going to freeze to death."

Their laughter seemed to echo through the air as the old family home came into view.

The pang in his chest became too real. He felt so raw, he pulled over unable to tear his gaze from the two-story white house.

Thank God he'd not have to go inside it. The real estate sign had a magnetic "Sold" sash across it.

Taylor pressed the gas pedal down and sped away from the house. It was better not to allow emotions to get the best of him. In a couple miles, he'd face Janice, his ex and who knew what that would bring.

THEIR MARRIAGE DID not withstand the double blow of the death of their two children and her parents.

His father-in-law had either had a heart attack or a brain embolism, which caused him to drive across the median and into oncoming traffic. They'd hit a gasoline tanker truck head on.

Along with everyone in their car, the accident also killed the truck driver and two other people in nearby cars when the truck's contents exploded, burning up everything and everyone.

The coroner had done her best to waylay their fears, explaining it was probable everyone had died instantly. But they knew there was no way to know for sure. Nightmares had tortured them nightly. Lack of sleep, guilt, worry, and stress lead to constant fights.

Taylor parallel parked in front of his ex sister-in-law's house. The blinds moved as someone looked out. Instead of going to the front door, he got out and stood by the truck.

He was not welcome there.

Janice's family blamed him for what had happened. It was he who was supposed to go pick the children up from visiting her parents a couple hours away.

Instead, he'd convinced his father-in-law to come up for a visit. Yeah, he'd not felt like making the drive.

So as far as Taylor knew, everyone in these situations had regrets and if-onlys. His however, was a doozy.

The garage door creaked and began its slow ascent. The automatic opener was in desperate need of oil, or replacement by the way it shook and groaned.

Finally, the sunlight allowed him to see her. Janice stood next to two boxes. Her arms crossed and face carefully schooled into a blank look.

"Hello." He had to clear his throat as the word stuck.

Instead of a greeting, she motioned to the boxes. "The movers came last week. I kept this stuff for you. Take it and go through it when you get a chance. Do what you want with it."

He looked at the boxes. The pitiful remains of two vibrant beautiful lives. At only eight and ten, Marcus and Briana were on the cusp of their existence and to them everything was new and fresh. But that all changed, their lives cut short because he would not drive to get them.

No matter how many times he was told by counselors and family, it was fate and feeling guilty would not change anything, the burden would remain. Until the day he died, Taylor would carry the heavy weight of knowing he could have kept his children and possibly his mother and father-in-law as well from dying.

"So, you're moving to Canada?" Taylor met her gaze, ensuring she looked at him. This was the woman he'd loved like no other, the mother of his children. They'd planned to grow old together, and she still meant a great deal to him. It was a cruel twist of destiny, because now they'd never see each other again.

"Yes." Her reply was breathless. "I am."

Instead of the deep feeling of love and need to be with her, that he expected, Janice brought memories of a different life and hopes they'd both one day move on.

He picked up the first box and placed it on the back seat of his truck and then returned for the second one. The boxes were heavy and he wondered what all was in them.

When he returned empty-handed, Janice held out a small rectangular box with a blue ribbon tied around it. "This is yours. It was going to be your Father's Day gift that year. I'd forgotten about it until I was cleaning things out and saw it."

A knot caught in his throat when he slipped the ribbon off and opened it up to reveal a handmade frame made from Popsicle sticks. In it was a picture of him and his children. They'd gone swimming that summer and Janice had snapped a picture of the kids hanging by his biceps. All three had almost identical wide grins and windblown hair.

"That was a good summer," Janice said, a slight curve to her lips. "We had fun that day."

Taylor nodded, words evading him for a moment. "Are you sure about this? About leaving? Do you think we…"

She began shaking her head as soon as he started talking and backed away toward the side door that would lead into the kitchen. "I think it's best if I never see you again. Goodbye Taylor."

"If you ever need anything…." He left the rest of the sentence unsaid as she went inside.

He remained standing with the picture in his hands and gaze on the door. It was over. Nothing could ever repair the damage. Her brown eyes had instantly brought back the image of Briana's long lashed ones. He was sure his hazel ones and cleft chin reminded Janice of Marcus' features.

"Goodbye," he whispered and turned away.

WHEN TAYLOR GOT home everything was dark, except for the light of the television screen.

From the couch with his legs stretched across the ottoman, Tobias lifted a beer in salute.

"What's up Cuz?"

He would have preferred to go straight to bed after

stashing the boxes in the corner of their large garage. "Not much."

Guns blazing, Bruce Willis appeared on the screen, his mouth sneering as he dove behind a barricade. The noise was a good distraction from Taylor's groan as he lowered to a chair.

"Long drive. Can't do those anymore without paying the price."

Tobias studied him for a long moment. "Eric said you haven't been to see the pain doctor."

He was too tired to hear the shit. "I'll have to go this week. Out of meds."

"Eric said you'd taken more than was probably prescribed when he stopped by."

Tobias was a huge guy. Not only because he was muscular from regular weight training, but at six-five, the wide-shouldered man towered over most people. The only one that could give Tobias a run for his money was Luke, his identical twin.

Of the three of them, Tobias was the lucky one. From the way he told it, he'd flirted his way to a cushy job when deployed to the Middle East. He'd not seen any action. Luke always argued his twin was lying, but it seemed Tobias was about as normal as brown gravy.

Some days, he was too normal. The only black spot in Tobias' past was a broken heart. And who the hell didn't go through that anyway?

In his cousin's case however, it seemed Tobias hadn't managed to get over it. Whenever he saw Victoria, his ex-fiancée, they got into an argument. Fought like cats and dogs if ever alone longer than a minute. Once she'd even rammed her car into his trunk in a fit of fury.

It was rather comical to see them go at it. It was obvious to everyone except the two idiots they were still in love.

"Since when have you and Eric become my health counselors? Nosy assholes." He stood.

Tobias narrowed his eyes, jaw tense. "When are you going?"

"Leave me the fuck alone Tobias. I don't need this shit right now." He considered that he'd been planning to take more than the recommended dosage that night from pills he'd coerced from the pharmacist in town. The guy would deduct the pills once he came back to pick up the prescription.

"Something else," Tobias said ignoring his glare. "Frank busted his arm today."

He turned to Tobias. Frank was a long-time worker and reliable ranch hand. "What happened?"

"Horse kicked him. It had to hurt like a mother. His arm was bent all back." Tobias demonstrated curving his arm up. "He'll be out of commission for at least a couple of months."

It was bad news. With the way his hip was hurting, Taylor had planned to take time to allow for downtime. Although he didn't ride a horse, the uneven terrain on the four-wheeler was not conducive with painful injuries.

"Can't you ask Luke to help out more? I feel like shit

lately."

Tobias groaned and slapped the couch arm. "That's why you need to go get seen by the doctor."

"I'll go tomorrow."

CHAPTER FOURTEEN

T HE RINGING OF the bell over the door of the shop made Allison jerk. She'd spent the night in her own apartment after two nights at Tori's. No one had seen anything of notice and Mindy's brother's body would be brought back from the coroner, which meant the funeral was about to take place that weekend.

With the suspect not being caught, it caused her fretful nights. She'd jarred awake with every sound until giving up as soon as the first bits of sunshine peeked over the horizon.

Eric Hamilton stalked in, making a beeline for the counter. She took a step backward at noting the crease between his brows.

"I thought you were staying at Tori's?"

"I did. I slept at Tori's for a couple of nights. Seriously Eric, I can't stay at other people's places indefinitely."

He didn't look convinced. "You got a security system?"

"Yes."

"A gun?"

"Yep."

He let out a long sigh. "You haven't seen that reporter guy again?"

"No, but he did stop by Tori's to eat and asked a couple questions."

Other than the height and broad shoulders, there was little resemblance between Eric and Taylor. Yet the Hamilton somber expression seemed to be a constant.

"My partner and I will continue patrolling the street. Don't hesitate to call if you hear or see anything. I don't care what time it is."

She'd not heard from Taylor since he'd texted to cancel coming over. "Have you heard from Taylor?"

Eric shrugged. "Nah. He went to Wyoming to see his ex." Seeming to realize his slip, he quickly began talking again. "I think the suspect will be apprehended shortly, so no need to be nervous. I will ask that you keep the front door locked. You can see customers coming. If it's a man by himself and you don't recognize him, lie and say you're closed for a few minutes.

Allison nodded and saluted. "Got it."

The corner of Eric's mouth twitched. "See that you follow orders."

After he left, a feeling of loneliness took over and Allison fought not to cry. Although she relished her freedom and independence, there were days she had a recurring fear. She be injured or killed and it would be days before anyone thought to check on her.

It was silly in the case of being dead of course. At that point, she'd not care one way or the other. However, what if she was stabbed by the man who'd killed Mindy's brother and could not call for help?

A single tear slipped down her cheek and she swiped it away angry with herself for being so silly.

It was the fact that Taylor was with his ex that caused all of these feelings. There was no use in denying how much it hurt that he'd left to see his ex-wife after being together. What would happen now? If they reconciled, he would probably move to Wyoming where he used to live.

Allison had no regrets about the sex. After all, she'd wanted the man all her life. And she'd hoped for it to happen. It felt silly now to think that the memory of it would suffice when in fact she wanted a lot more than damn memories.

A soft song played in the background filling her shop while two gray-haired women walked by deep into a lively conversation. Across the street, a woman bundled her children into a car. Life continued in Laurel Creek.

Thank goodness for that.

LEAH BURST INTO the shop that afternoon, her gaze pinpointing Allison. While Allison rang up a customer who'd purchased several arrangements and a tray of chocolates, Leah paced with ill concealed impatience.

Allison helped the woman carry her purchases out to her car all the while giving her friend questioning looks.

As much as she wanted to know what was up with Leah, she took the time to ensure her customer's flowers were stable in the car.

When she turned to go back inside Leah was standing beside the door. She yanked Allison by the arm and pulled her inside.

"I can't believe Taylor left you alone," she said, screaming it more than a little angry. "What the hell is wrong with him?" Angry mottled streaks of red crossed Leah's face and neck. "Oh and I'm totally pissed at Luke and Tobias. One of them should have taken over. They are all in the dog house."

"The twins were gone to the auction…" Allison began defending only to be cut off.

"They got back two days ago. One of them should have made sure you were okay after Taylor left."

Allison sniffed and hugged Leah. "I'm fine. I stayed at Tori's for a couple of nights. Let's have tea. You need to calm down."

Both took a breath. Leah swallowed and looked at Allison for a long time. "I was terrified for you when Luke told me he'd not come to check on you. The dorks counted on Eric to watch over you."

"It's okay." Allison smiled, happy to have company, her spirits immediately lifted.

"Oh and I am not sure what's going on with Taylor. Tobias told Luke he packed up a bag and left early this morning. He didn't say anything other than he needed to take care of some personal stuff. Tobias is livid."

Perhaps being stabbed by the killer would have hurt less. Although Allison suspected it could happen, hearing it was a totally different story. Taylor was probably working things out with his ex.

"Really?" It was all she could think to say. "Why is Tobias mad?"

Leah waved Allison to the table. "Sit down, I have to keep moving." She poured hot water from the electric teapot into cups. After carefully measuring loose tea into small tea bags, she plopped them into each cup.

It took a lot of willpower not to hurry her along, but Allison remained sitting. She refused to cry or allow emotion to take over.

Finally Leah sat down. "Taylor is not doing well. He has been taking a lot of pain medication for his hip. He stopped going to pain management. He was supposed to go and get seen this week."

"He may have gone," Allison replied. "Who knows?"

Leah shrugged. "Maybe, but it seems crazy to just pack and leave if that was the case."

There was a moment of hesitation when Allison's cell phone dinged. "I have an appointment in ten minutes. A bride and her mother."

"No problem, I won't be in the way. I'll just set up over there," Leah said pointing to the corner behind the chocolate counter."

"Set up what?"

"My computer. I'm working from here until they apprehend the killer. And I'm sleeping here too." Leah jumped to her feet. "Help me get my stuff."

She couldn't help but smile as she followed her bossy friend outside.

"WHAT?" LEAH SCREAMED. "You slept with Taylor and are just now telling me about it."

That evening, they sat on the couch, each one with a laptop browsing the Internet while chatting. Leah pushed hers off and leaned forward. "You better put that computer down and look at me."

"Fine." Allison prolonged it on purpose just to annoy Leah. "It was the second night he was here. We started making out and one thing led to another."

Leah's gaze searched her face and a slow curve of her lips turned into a wide smile. "So, was it good?"

"Amazing." Allison sighed. "Best sex ever."

"Ooooh." With a dramatic gesture, Leah crossed both hands over her chest and swayed. "Those Hamiltons have it going on."

"Yep." Her chest constricted at the fact she'd never sleep with him again. "Got my wish after so long."

"Damn and now this." Leah blew out a frustrated breath. "He sucks."

"Hey, maybe when he went to Wyoming, he and the ex realized they wanted to be together."

Leah didn't look convinced. "Then again, he may

have headed to the woods to live in a cave."

"That I doubt." Allison couldn't help but laugh at the thought while at the same time something about the entire thing bothered her. He didn't seem the impulsive type. "I hope he's okay. Maybe I'll call him, you know, pretend I don't know he left."

"Good idea." Leah's gaze moved to the cell phone on her side table. "Do it now."

Although she wanted to call and every fiber of her being demanded it, the thought he'd actually answer kept her from doing so. No, it was best to wait.

Taylor Hamilton needed to get away. Whatever his reasoning, if he'd wanted to talk to her, he would have.

"I'll wait. I can't do it now."

CHAPTER FIFTEEN

T HE NOISE OF the talking heads on the television in the hotel room barely drowned out the inhuman sounds that came from the man huddled on the floor. His back to the corner, Taylor let every emotion loose, even after his throat became hoarse from it.

No one in the cheap, rent by the hour motel would come check to ensure someone wasn't being killed. In this area of Billings, people kept to themselves. Better to let the owner or the cops find out than be tied to any kind of crime.

When one needed total privacy, this was the place. He'd paid for a week in advance just to ensure it. Told the manager no maid service and the man hadn't even blinked at the request.

He was barefoot and had worn the same t-shirt for three days now. Probably stunk too since he'd not bathed for just as long. The last thing Taylor gave a fuck about right then was hygiene.

The faces he'd blocked for years appeared over and

over again. Each memory of time spent with his son and daughter sliced at him, like a sword across the chest. The pain was so vivid now, he was shocked to have lived through it then.

Yes he'd grieved along with Janice and the family. He'd been strong for them, especially Janice who'd gone into a silent shock for days.

While going through the process of repairing their life, he'd lost sight of needing to go through accepting his children and wife's parents were really gone forever.

The picture of the three of them, his son, daughter and him at the lake was on the still made bed. The smiling faces a reminder of a life that didn't even seem his.

The man in the picture with the broad smile, holding his kids up, was not him. It was someone he'd once been.

Denial was the only way he'd moved on. It was his weapon of choice, the only way he'd dealt with losing his kids, his wife and finally his career.

The last few days, the pains in his hip were welcomed. Each throb and ache was punishment for surviving. It was his sentence for not going to get his children that day and Taylor had no wish to relinquish it.

The cellphone dinged and like the many times before, Taylor ignored it. It was surprising the damn cell phone was still charged with all the dinging and shit. He'd not had the energy to get to it and turn it off. Eventually it would go dead.

His eyes were swollen and dry. His eyelids felt like sandpaper rubbing across the surface when he opened them.

Prying his eyes open, Taylor cringed.

With each hour that passed, the pain from his left hip down the leg became more unbearable until Taylor groaned with each breath. So, this was what he'd been missing by popping the pain pills like Tic-Tacs.

The visit to a doctor, whenever he decided to go, wasn't going to bring good news. He didn't need a PhD to know surgery was on the horizon for him. It would be either number ten or twelve. He'd lost count during the haze of going under over and over in the aftermath of the shooting.

Recovery had been worse than the actual shooting. Maybe it was because he'd gone into shock and lost consciousness quite a bit. After the surgery, he'd been wide-awake for each and every torturous second. Tears had poured down his face as he'd taken his first pain-filled steps. The physical therapy was a barely tolerable event for many weeks.

The sunlight that trickled through the faded curtains turned to shadows as the third day ended. His stomach had stopped growling. Hunger now replaced with pangs of hollowness.

Yet Taylor could not be motivated to move. At this point he'd consider wetting his pants instead of having to deal with the agony of having to stand up.

Sitting too long did that to an old injury. It turned

stiff and painful, which was the reason every morning was not exactly a fun time.

There was mumbling outside and he stared at the door. The manager was talking to someone. He couldn't make out the other voice, but it was deep. Probably it was someone wanting to get into the room next door or something. He lowered his head and squeezed his eyes closed. One more day, maybe two and he'd go directly to the pain management place to see the doctor.

Too bad a hip couldn't be amputated.

"Open the door or I'll kick it down," a familiar voice said from the other side. "I mean it Taylor. Open the fucking door." It was either Luke or Tobias on the other side. Probably Luke from the way his deep voice lowered when threatening.

The fucker was intimidating as hell. Most people gave him a wide berth whenever he passed them.

Unlike most people, Taylor didn't give a rat's ass what the guy threatened him with.

"Fuck you," Taylor replied. The hoarseness of his voice was just above a whisper. Damn. So much for sounding like "I'm all right."

Bang. Bang. Whoosh.

There were two kicks and daylight streamed in around the huge asshole who stood in the entrance. He wore a worn baseball cap and wraparound sunglasses, which meant he'd ridden his motorcycle. The heavy boots crunched over splinters of wood as he stalked toward him.

The manager screamed that he'd found the key and telling Luke he'd pay for damages and calling the cops.

"Go ahead. I'm sure they'll find more than a dying man on the premises," Luke said not sounding at all concerned.

Taylor lowered his head and pressed his forehead onto his forearms that were across his bent right leg. It was impossible to do the same with his throbbing left one.

"Get the fuck out Luke. I swear if you say one fucking thing, I'm going to kick your ass."

His cousin turned around and closed the door. Of course the locks didn't work and Luke had to lift it a bit to make it close, but it stayed, which was good.

Boots came into view and Luke lowered to his haunches. He pressed a couple of fingers to the side of Taylor's neck, and then swiped a big ass palm across his forehead.

Then without a word, Luke stood and then settled onto the bed. On his back with arms behind his head, he stared up at the ceiling. Apparently his cousin was there for the long run and ensured to be comfortable.

WHEN TAYLOR WOKE up, he was on his side. He was still on the floor but had a blanket thrown over him. The combination of a fresh shot of pain and having to piss woke him with a start. He must have groaned because Luke was at his side immediately.

"I'll help you up."

Thank fuck Luke was so strong otherwise he wouldn't have made it up. Luke slipped both hands under his arms and pulled him upright.

"Augh!" Taylor cried out and would have fallen sideways when he tried to stand on his left foot if it wasn't for his cousin.

The mercurial taste of blood filled his mouth when he bit down on his lip to keep from screaming.

He hissed when attempting to take another step. "Damn it."

"I'll help you to the bathroom, but I'm not holding your dick."

Taylor slid him a glance. "And here I was hoping you would."

Half dragged to the bathroom, by the time they made it, Taylor was panting. Three days without food and water was not exactly a good combination. Add to that great combo not being able to move and boom, you got a dead man walking.

"I'll be back in five," Luke said after helping Taylor to sit on the bed. "Don't rush off anywhere." He jiggled Taylor's truck keys and slipped them in his pocket.

Although he rolled his eyes at Luke's back, he realized how damn lucky he was to have family that gave a shit about him.

Luke would return with food and drink and then he'd wait until Taylor was good and ready to leave. His cousin was that kind of guy. He'd stay for weeks if needed. He'd not try to do any kind of pep talk, nor would he force Taylor to say a word. Instead his quiet, steady presence would be a reassurance.

Although Luke had lost soldiers and good friends in war, Taylor didn't dare try to compare whose loss was worse. He'd venture to bet his was greater. Either way, they both had some horrible shit to deal with. Although it was a bond of sorts, it was one he'd gladly have passed on.

At the moment, he couldn't think of anyone who could be a better person to be there for him.

Reaching for the picture frame on the bed, once again the wide grins of his kids making his heart wrench and every fiber of his being ache. How he missed those kids.

He'd give anything to hear his daughter's sweet giggle or his boy's smart-ass remarks. Tears slipped down his cheeks unchecked and he let out a long breath and held the picture against his chest.

CHAPTER SIXTEEN

A S THE WEEKS passed, Allison settled into a routine of sorts. A strange numbness of going through the motions took over and she hated every minute of it.

Even after Eric came to inform her the suspect had been arrested and confessed to the murder, it was hard to sleep some nights.

In an effort to shake the strange emptiness, she went to spend a week visiting Jaden and his girlfriend in Seattle. The visit although enjoyable, was overshadowed by not knowing what was going on with Taylor.

The family had been very silent about where he'd gone or what had happened to him. All she heard from Leah was that Taylor had gone to Billings for surgery on his hip and was living there with family while going to physical therapy.

It helped somewhat to know he and his ex had not reconciled. If anyone knew where Taylor had gone to after Wyoming, they'd not said a word.

Right after returning to Laurel Creek from Seattle,

Allison was swamped with holiday orders and upcoming festivities. She'd joined the town's decorating committee. Along with Tori and Mindy, they'd oversee the street and city hall decorations as well as manage decorating the town's Christmas tree.

Now as she primped in the mirror, her gaze moved to the bed. Each time the picture of making love with Taylor struck her and her heart warmed. The time with him was special and she'd never regret it. However, today she was going on a date. It was time to move on.

Hope that a relationship with Taylor would blossom had been just that, wishful thinking and nothing more.

The man had not bothered to call her once in almost six weeks. So yes, she understood he was no doubt going through the painful process of recovery and physical therapy. However, when a person cared at least a little about furthering a romantic connection, some effort was required.

Her date, a veterinarian named Ben had asked her out after stopping by one day to pick up flowers for his sister.

Ben was cocky, bold and fun. They'd spoken over the phone a couple of times and he'd made her laugh. It was obvious by the mentions of "having a good time" Ben was after a casual relationship.

Needing to move on from a long-term situation with David and her tryst with Taylor, something casual was just what she needed. It was best to ease back into the future by dating and being more realistic in what kind of men were out there.

The ding of the doorbell made her heart jump and Allison giggled at the childish reaction. What the hell was wrong with her?

She opened the door to find Ben wearing a blue and white plaid shirt, jeans and a sexy smirk.

Caught checking him out, she shrugged. "I'm ready." She stepped through the door and ensured it was locked.

He didn't take her arm, instead walked ahead and opened the passenger door of his Jeep. "Hope you like steak."

A flat gaze met her questioning look. "I do. Where are we going?"

"It's a surprise." The vehicle came to life and Ben guided it down the center of town and kept going.

"I assume you do a lot of on-call visits around here." Allison decided to make conversation since her nerves were beginning to take over.

"Yeah, it's hard to get horses to come in for appointments," Ben replied with a smile. "You have a pet?"

"No. I like dogs and cats. After my cat died last year, I haven't gotten another pet. Thinking about it."

They continued with small talk until arriving at a ranch. To the side of a large home was a group of people gathered around a large bonfire.

Allison instantly relaxed. "Whose house is this?"

"Eric Hamilton's. We usually get together a couple of weekends a month and hang out before it gets too cold."

Her blood froze. If Taylor was there, she was going to die. Then again, what difference did it make? She'd not heard boo from him since he'd gone. It's not like they'd made some sort of commitment.

Ben was looking at her as if expecting a reply. It was then she realized he'd asked her something.

"It's already freezing," she said shaking her head. "Good thing they have a bonfire."

"Are you okay? Disappointed? I thought this would be a good first date. No pressure."

"I'm sorry. I was looking to see who all was here." She met his gaze. "It's a perfect first date. Great surprise."

She recognized Eric, Ernest who was Eric's older brother, and Ernest's partner Henry. There were a couple of women; one of them was Mindy, the café owner. She was surprised to see Mindy out so soon after her brother's death. Then again, it was good. Grieving took a lot out of a person and being out with people was healthy.

Allison waited for Ben to get a cooler out of the back of the Jeep and they walked up to the bonfire together. Other than the five people present, there wasn't anyone else around that she could see.

After being introduced to the second woman, Felicia, who gave her a quizzical look, everyone settled into chairs. Ben had thoughtfully brought two lawn chairs.

"Need to grab some beer from inside." Eric motioned Ben over to help and they went inside.

Ernest began laughing at something Felicia said and

both looked to the others.

"What's so funny?" Henry asked.

"Eric's lame excuse for talking to Ben alone. The beer cooler is right here," Felicia said looking first to the blue container and then to Allison. "Probably wants to grill him."

For some reason, Allison took an immediate dislike to Felicia. It was as if the woman held some sort of secret that involved her and she was relishing in it.

Mindy smiled at Allison. "I'm glad you're here. I was wondering if either you or Leah would be here since Luke was here earlier."

"I didn't know about it until just when I arrived. It's our first date and he thought it would be relaxing to come hang out. Not so formal.

"What a great idea," Ernest the social butterfly said, not hiding the fact he had been eavesdropping. "Ben is a great guy."

Felicia studied her for a moment. "I thought you were dating Taylor Hamilton."

Taken aback, all Allison could do was look to the others. Everyone looked to her with interest, even Mindy. "We umm...hung out after the murder for a couple days. That's it. We're just friends. Known each other since high school."

At her statement, everyone except Felicia seemed convinced. Who was this woman anyway? "And how do you know everyone?" Allison asked.

"I worked with Taylor. Same precinct. We were

partners. I have family here in town too."

The woman got up and went to the cooler. Mindy gave Allison a questioning look and she shrugged in return.

Ben and Eric came back outside. They carried a tray and a platter piled with meat. Talking, they went to the grill and Felicia went inside.

"She's pretty," Mindy said. "I wonder why she's here and Taylor isn't? She is definitely staking her territory by the way she said "partners", as if it meant more than just co-workers."

"Yep, I got that," Allison replied. "Loud and clear."

WHILE THE FOOD cooked, Henry set up a small card table where he put paper plates and eating utensils. He then went inside and returned with a salad.

"Food's almost ready. Someone go help Taylor," Eric called out. "He's probably asleep in front of the television."

Allison's stomach sunk. Taylor was there? She and Mindy exchanged "WTF" looks.

"Probably need two people," Ernest said, following Henry inside.

Moments later, the guys flanked Taylor. He walked on his own with a cane until getting to the top step.

He grumbled when the guys slipped arms under his and carried him down the steps. "Damn I could've done it. I swear this family gets the prize for overbearing assholes of the year."

His upper torso swayed to the left and right with each step as he leaned heavily on his cane and walked to the table.

He wore some sort of brace that kept his left side steady. There was a thick belt around his waist and straps around his thigh all the way down his leg.

He'd not noticed her, too busy glaring at Henry and Earnest who seemed to enjoy ribbing him.

"Want a beer?" Felicia walked up beside him so he was forced to remain turned away from where Allison sat.

"Sure, I'd love that and two shots of whiskey. But can't take anything with all the damn meds I'm on."

When he turned and finally saw her, his eyes widened just for a second.

She couldn't tell what he thought as he masked his reaction rather quickly.

CHAPTER SEVENTEEN

T HINGS JUST KEPT getting better. Taylor eyed the front door and considered the distance and his ability to get in his truck.

Eric parked it parallel to the porch to make it easier for him. However, with the way his family hovered, he'd not make it that far before one of them stopped him.

Earlier when Ernest and Henry had come inside, he thought he'd heard Allison's name. He'd been half asleep trying to ignore Felicia's running commentary of the game on the television.

So, was she Ben's date?

When Ben sat down next to her with his plate of food, it was obvious they were definitely there together.

And he wanted to punch the guy's lights out.

"First date," Earnest mumbled, placing a plate loaded with potato salad, steak and a sausage in front of him and settling down next to him with one just as full. "Why the hell would he take a girl to a group thing on a first date? Not like him. She must be special to him."

Through narrowed eyes, he saw Allison laugh at something Ben said and they shared it with Mindy who joined in. Eric lowered to sit beside Mindy, whom Taylor knew his cousin was interested in.

That left him with Felicia if everyone was partnered up. Which he decided was not a thing.

Seeming to sense his aggravation, Felicia met his gaze and then looked to where Ben and Allison sat. "Interesting group of people. Maybe next time I'll bring a date. Seems like this is a pairs thing."

Taylor shrugged and began eating. Despite the annoyance of seeing Allison out with his friend, the food was amazing.

After eating, Henry, the self appointed social director, got everyone to agree to a board game. The only two not playing were him and Allison, who came and sat next to him.

"How's the healing coming along? Her husky voice traveled straight through him. "I got updates from Leah, but haven't heard about anything lately."

She didn't seem angry. Her long fingers trailed down the side of the beer bottle as she watched the game.

"Slow going. The physical therapy is a barrel of fun."

"Hmmm. It always seems to be the worst part. When Jaden, my stepson, had a car accident, he messed up his knee and said the pain of the injury was less than the pain during the physical therapy."

He'd not heard much about her stepson, other than knowing the boy was at least twenty-five and on his own.

He didn't remember much about Allison's life after high school. He was already in college by the time she graduated and since he'd gone from there to Billings, he'd missed out on knowing whom she married.

"Your ex-husband live here in Laurel Creek?"

"No. He lives in Seattle. Actually, Jaden lives there too."

She laughed when someone made a mistake costing a point and high-fived Ben. The throaty sound made him want to high five the guy too, fist to face.

Before the game ended, he got up. Immediately, Ernest and Henry rushed to his aid making him want to growl. Instead, he let them help him up the stairs and away from Allison Brennan.

"KINDA THOUGHT YOU'D punch Ben out a couple of times. Maybe it's a good thing you can't move too fast." Eric laughed. It was almost midnight and everyone except Felicia, who was bunking there, had left.

"What are you talking about?" Taylor stared at the television. It may as well have been Sesame Street, as he'd not paid the movie any attention.

Eric sat down and put a foot up on the ottoman. "You didn't bother hiding your emotions well. Kinda disappointing for an old cop."

"I feel like shit. That's the emotion I have."

"Bull. Shit."

"What about Mindy? You waiting on a meteor to fly

by with a banner? You moving awful slow Cuz."

Eric let out a long breath. "Her brother just died and besides, she seems kinda gun shy. Every time I am near her, she gets all stiff and shit."

"You're an idiot."

"Takes one to know one." Eric looked to the back of the house where Felicia was. "What's up with her?"

"She's being a protector of some kind. As a matter of fact, I think she is interested in Ben and tonight didn't exactly give her any warm fuzzies."

Eric began laughing and soon Taylor joined in. "We're a bunch of idiots. All the dynamics going on, it's crazy."

Eric chuckled a few times. "So you like Allison, but she was on a date with Ben who Felicia digs and Mindy gets twitchy around me. The only couple that had their shit together tonight were the two dudes. That's hilarious."

"Right." Taylor didn't find it as hilarious as he would have liked. As much as he'd wanted to contact Allison, it had been too hard. Dealing with all the shit that hit him in the face after seeing Janice and then the surgery had left him drained.

Although he'd thought of Allison all the time, he wasn't sure it was a good idea to contact her and give her any ideas regarding a future.

The doctors were hesitant to give him an "everything will be fine" response. His pelvic bone had to be reconstructed. That was followed by two weeks of bed rest to allow the bone to heal. Then there was the wonderful carnival ride of going back in when something wasn't quite right.

The shattered bone wasn't cooperating. He'd then gone through hip replacement and while they were in there, they'd reinforced his femur.

"You're a lucky man. The bullets hit everything but the main artery," the docs had spouted.

Yeah lucky. The lottery prize was a lifetime of pain and limping. Not to mention the fact any kind of sex would have to be in some kind of alternate position. Which position exactly, he wasn't quite sure of yet.

Eric's head lulled to the side and he jerked awake. "Hey, I need to help you get settled. I'm about to pass out."

Although Taylor grumbled about it, he had a great family. As he closed his eyes in the double recliner he'd been sleeping in, his last thoughts were of how to make love to Allison.

THE NEXT DAY it was quiet. Eric was gone to work and Felicia had left early that morning.

The only one in the house besides him was Eric's German Shepard, Scout.

The dog was trained so well, it was as if a person was actually there to keep an eye on him. The huge animal laid in front of the fireplace his head on his front paws. Although his eyes closed from time to time, they would open and look to him.

Obviously, the command had been for Scout to watch after him. It was his third day there. He'd come to Eric's instead of his own home because it was the only house with a recliner. He couldn't sleep in a regular bed and get out of it by himself.

The way he saw it, one bachelor pad was as good as another. It wasn't like he was going to spend time doing much more than surfing the Internet and watching television. Thankfully, the newest edition of Assassin's Creed was out, so that gave him plenty to keep his mind busy with.

Although it hurt like a motherfucker at physical therapy, whenever he was still the hip area was pretty much pain free now. He wasn't steady while walking yet, but it didn't hurt as much anymore.

It would be weeks before he was considered fully recovered by the doctors and given the go ahead to return to work on the ranch. With Scout along and a walker, he was able to make it to his truck and drive to his appointments, which pissed off the doctors.

He went to physical therapy three times a week. Each time he'd start sweating before making it through the door. Today however, all he had to look forward to was gaming and leftovers. In his book, it was as perfect as one could get.

THE BELL OVER the door at the café dinged and Mindy

looked up as Eric walked in. Immediately she stiffened. It was so annoying how nervous he made her.

For the first time in her life, she was attracted to a man to the point of distraction and this was how she reacted. What the hell was wrong with her?

With jerky movements, she managed to ring up a customer and waited for the man to pick up the cup and plate with a muffin instead of her usual motions of lifting and handing the items over. It was best not to drench a customer in boiling hot coffee.

"Good morning," Eric said glancing in her direction before studying the menu. "Got any cinnamon raisin bagels?"

"Sorry, we sold out."

"Got any pumpkin pie?" He continued staring at the menu.

"We never sell it." She narrowed her eyes at him and was about to ask what he was up to but he interrupted.

"I really would love a slice of cheesecake."

Mindy looked to her display and to him. "I have croissants, oatmeal muffins, cheese Danishes and white, wheat or rye toast."

"Ever consider adding to your menu?" Eric glanced at her and back at the menu. "It's quite limited."

Annoyed, she huffed, "We make breakfast and lunch sandwiches. On Wednesdays, we make quiche. It's what we do. Is there anything on the menu you'd like?"

This time he met her gaze. His hazel eyes lingered on hers and then trailed to her lips. "Actually, no I don't see what I really want on the menu."

Someone seated giggled and Eric turned to the older woman and winked. When he looked back to her, Mindy was sure her face was bright red.

"So, coffee and a sausage and cheese croissant as usual then." She didn't ask, but stated what he usually ate and turned to the small window where her employee was slicing meat. "Sausage and cheese croissant please Jenny."

She took longer than necessary to pour his coffee into the insulated mug he always carried since her hand was shaking. Then before facing him, she took a slow breath hoping he didn't notice.

Eric was speaking to the woman when she turned. "So you see, I think Miss Mindy here doesn't like me much. So I try to annoy her as much as possible."

"That's not true. I don't dislike you." Mindy rolled her eyes.

"She's lying," he told the delighted woman. "She's being nice because you're here."

Unable to figure out what exactly was happening, Mindy could only remain transfixed as he bent to look at a picture the woman showed him on her phone. The woman explained that her now deceased husband had been a police officer.

Mindy had to admit that Eric was mouthwateringly attractive. His rear pointed to her, she allowed her gaze to linger before trailing it up past his slender waist to the broad back. In his gear, the man could stop traffic without moving a finger.

"Up!" Jenny screamed more than said and plopped the sandwich on the counter.

"Do you want this to go?" Mindy asked Eric's back.

He neared and picked up the coffee cup. "Yep. Thanks."

Although she wanted him to leave so her breathing would normalize, she'd hoped not to have to wrap up the meal and bag it.

Thankfully a couple walked in and engaged Eric in a conversation and she was distracted enough to get his food bagged.

When he reached for the bag, his fingers touched the back of her hand and Eric met her gaze. "See you tomorrow."

"If only I was twenty years younger," the older woman said with a sigh. "He's a cutie, isn't he?" She smiled at Mindy.

"Yes ma'am. He is."

And he was a flirt who enjoyed making her uncomfortable.

CHAPTER EIGHTEEN

Allison wasn't sure what to do when a car pulled up in front of her shop. Moments later, Felicia's face was visible as the woman leaned to the passenger side to look at her window.

Great. Just what she needed, some sort of jealous drama. Although Allison wasn't sure what Felicia was upset about. She'd pretty much stayed away from Taylor the entire night except for a few moments during the board game.

The woman's sharp gaze met hers as she walked in. "I am not here to buy anything."

"Okay," Allison said drawing out the 'O'. "What can I do for you?"

"Look, I feel as if I was less than friendly last night. But my protective side comes out when it comes to Taylor. I thought y'all had something going on, so when you showed up with Ben…"

"Ben and I are just friends. Nothing will develop there. It's not me you should be protecting Taylor from.

He's not interested in me in the least."

Her right eyebrow lifted, as she seemed to consider what to say next. "So you and Ben…nada?"

"Nope. But it was a great first date." It was interesting when the woman frowned at her insinuating there could be a second. "Can I ask why you're so invested in this?"

She let out a breath. "Just what I said. Taylor's going through a rough time… Making sure things don't get complicated for him."

Although it was none of the woman's business and her visit made little sense, Allison decided it was best to tell it like it was.

"Things between Taylor and I fizzled. Not because of me, but because of him. I had not heard from him in almost two months. So up until last night we'd not spoken. Honestly, I don't expect to in the future either. If he's pining or interested in anyone, I can guarantee you it's not me."

Felicia's one shoulder shrug annoyed Allison. "Yeah, well, I see things differently. Maybe you should talk to Eric. See you around," Felicia said waving her hand dismissively over her shoulder as she walked out.

One thing was for sure, she and Felicia would never be best friends. Allison hated people who spoke in riddles. Why the hell would she speak to Eric? If anything, there were already too many people all up in her business.

LATER THAT AFTERNOON, just before closing, her cell phone dinged. Leah was inviting her for dinner. For a few moments she considered declining, but her friend was an amazing cook and her current plans for dinner were a bowl of pasta with butter in front of the television. So she texted back she'd be there and bring salad.

THROUGH THE WINDSHIELD, Hamilton ranch came into view and as Allison passed Taylor's house, she recalled those innocent days back when she was twelve. He'd been her girlish crush. Taylor was the boy who haunted her every daydream and late-night musings.

Something crossed the road, she didn't see much more than a large shadow before swerving to miss it. The car went sideways when she over corrected and before she could turn the wheel, she slammed into some trees.

The airbag deployed slamming her in the face and everything went fuzzy. It made no sense, what happened? Allison attempted to catch her breath, but it was hard to. Her eyelids fell and she attempted to open her eyes only to fail. Finally the need to keep them closed was too strong to resist.

"ALLISON?" EVERYTHING WAS hazy, but Taylor's voice was clear as a bell. "Don't move. Someone's coming." His hand touched the side of her face. "You banged your head pretty good."

"Damn badger," she muttered.

"What?"

"Something ran across the road. I think it was a badger or a dog." She grimaced and turned to look at him all the while blinking. "I'm okay. Just a bit woozy."

"I called for an ambulance." His face finally came into focus. The car's lights were still on and the engine continued running.

"I should cut off the engine…"

"Don't. They told me not to let you move in case of a spinal injury."

Allison knew her eyes rounded as she wiggled her toes. "I can move my toes." She tightened and relaxed her knees. "I think I'm okay. I don't want to go anywhere in an ambulance. That's overkill."

He looked back toward the road. "I saw your car when I was driving home just now."

"Should you be driving?"

He didn't reply, but instead turned to look to his right. "That's probably Luke and Leah. I called them when I saw your car."

Although not too far off the road, it had to have been hard for Taylor to manage to get there. "You shouldn't be here. You could fall and reinjure yourself. Make sure to wait for Luke to get here before moving."

"Kinda bossy for someone who just crashed into a tree, or three."

"Yeah well, I don't think my head bump is anywhere as bad as what you're rocking there guy."

He shrugged, looking away. "Over here," he called out and waved. "Bring a flashlight."

Within minutes not only were Luke and Leah taking turns staring at her, but also the paramedics arrived and strapped her onto a flat board. As they carried her to the ambulance, Taylor stood with Luke watching.

Leah walked along beside her. "I'm coming with you. Do you want me to call Jaden?"

"You don't have to, but thanks. Let's wait until they find out nothing's wrong and then I'll call him."

IT TOOK OVER three hours and many grumblings later before the doctor pronounced her with a light concussion. He reluctantly agreed to her going home as long as Leah promised to keep an eye on her.

Allison was bundled into Taylor's truck, which for some reason was outside when she was discharged.

"I am so hungry," Allison whined, not caring if she sounded like a five-year-old. "I can't believe I trashed my car. I hope Leah has leftovers."

"Since she's been at the hospital the entire time, I'm sure she does. Pretty certain she'll feed us when we get there. Whether we want to eat or not."

She was sporting a heck of a lump on her forehead and the doctor warned she'd have two black eyes by morning from the airbag hitting the glasses she'd been wearing.

They drove in silence for the first fifteen or so

minutes. Allison couldn't think of anything to say to him. Instead she went through a list of things she'd have to do to deal with the accident.

"I'm sorry I didn't call you." Taylor's features were unreadable thanks to the darkness. The lights from the dashboard were not enough for her to make out any expression.

Allison wanted to slap him. This was not exactly the time for the conversation. She was starving, had a headache, and was worried about her car. Not to mention Jaden threatening to come get her and bring her to live in Seattle, as if she were ancient. At forty-three, she still had at least another forty years before someone could claim she was too old to live alone.

But she supposed to a kid in his twenties, she was old. Her lips curved at her stepson demanding a video conversation so he could make sure she was truly alive. Thank goodness the black eyes had not made an appearance yet.

"Between personal shit and the surgery, I wasn't in any shape to do more than feel sorry for myself," Taylor continued, seeming to take her silence for not being convinced he meant well.

Allison touched his forearm. "You were not under any obligation to do so. Leah kept me informed of your progress. Seems like you've gone through a lot." *I wanted to be there for you.*

He'd not wanted her there and that was what bothered her. When a person cares, they want them there during the worst times. At least that's how she felt.

He turned to her for a second then back to the road. "I don't take what happened between us lightly. Don't ever think I do."

What the hell did that mean? Allison opened her mouth to ask, but couldn't come up with the phrasing. "I don't think you do. Hell what am I saying? I don't know what you think."

The truck swayed side to side over the uneven terrain of the shoulder. Silence filled the space when Taylor cut off the engine and turned to her. "Will you accept my apology? I've wanted to come see you and speak to you in person. I hate texting."

A shiver went through her at his scrutiny. The injuries and hunger replaced by something else. "I do, although I feel you don't owe me one."

His lips curved. "I can't stop thinking about us. The way you looked when I made love to you."

Her sharp intake of breath was the only sound for a few moments. Taylor cupped her nape and pulled her closer.

The kiss was soft at first and grew harder, making them both breathless between each press. He undid his seatbelt to allow closeness and Allison dug her fingers into his thick shoulder needing even more.

Trailing his lips to her temple, Taylor pressed the softest of kisses to her bruise. "I can't do much right now Allison. It's not fair to ask anything of you right now." They were cheek to cheek as he spoke into her ear, his deep voice sending chills down Allison's spine.

"What?" She pushed at his chest to look up at him.

CHAPTER NINETEEN

ALLISON PINNED HIM with a glare. She was beautiful when angry, he wanted to argue with her just to see her eyes shine and little nose perk. "For your information, when a person is sick or going through a rough time that is when you find out who is truly in your corner. Did you not see how your family rallies around you? They are spoiling you rotten. The guys won't even let you go down a set of stairs."

She huffed, catching a breath and he pressed a kiss to her lips only for her to shove him away again.

It was hard to keep from smiling.

"Furthermore," she continued. "I wanted to be there. If I truly mattered to you, you'd have wanted me there. So don't blow air up my ass because you want to get laid or something."

When he leaned in to kiss her again, this time she shoved him away harder and then she covered her mouth with both hands. "Oh shit. Did I hurt you?"

This time he grinned. "No."

"What's so funny?" She leaned forward and narrowed her eyes. "Why are you grinning?"

Of course this was not the time to fight with her. He had something serious to tell her. But first he had to calm her down. "Look. I am an idiot. That's established. I did want you there, but no man wants the woman he cares for seeing him like that."

"Ugh," Allison said crossing her arms. With her tumble of curls in disarray, she looked like an angry fairy. Soft and feminine, while at the same time not going to allow him to get away with much. She was the perfect woman for him. Which was why letting her go wasn't going to be easy.

He started up the truck and drove the last couple of miles to Luke and Leah's place.

Both remained silent as they pulled into the driveway. He honked a couple times and turned to her. "I better stay in the truck, can't be much help if I fall on my ass."

For a long moment they looked at each other without speaking until the front door opened and Luke rushed over to help. "Hey Cuz." Luke looked at Taylor. "I'll help you once I get Allison in the house."

"I don't need help." Allison pushed the truck door open and got out. After a glare, she hurried inside.

Luke followed her progress before turning to him. "What did you do?"

"I have no idea."

His cousin chuckled. "Sounds familiar. Leah says you

have to come in and eat."

"What is it with women? They run us like little boys," Taylor grumbled as Luke helped him get out of the truck.

"Yep." Luke's reply didn't go past the one word. Taylor hobbled to the front door leaning heavily on his cane. And wasn't that just a sexy picture.

He looked to Allison once inside, who pointedly ignored him. Interesting how it made him fell better that she didn't seem to care about his cane or the new pronounced limp. Nope, she wasn't about to let any of his issues get in the way of being angry with him.

"Come on everyone, sit down. I know you're starving, cause I am." Leah kept an eye on Allison who carried two bowls to the table.

"We're having chili," Luke informed Taylor as he lowered to sit. "And cornbread."

Although Allison and Leah spoke throughout dinner, with interjections by Luke and Taylor, Allison would not look directly at him. Nor did she engage in conversation with him whenever he made a comment.

Somehow he'd make the time, get her alone to talk to her once she felt better. This day was bad enough for her. He'd been an idiot by bringing up the subject of not contacting her. Wow twice in a row, he was on a roll. All aboard the Idiot's Train, he was the conductor.

"So Taylor, you need to stay here tonight. You look dead on your feet." Leah studied his face, concern etched on her features.

"I'm off to sleep." Allison stood and after plopping her bowl on the counter hightailed it out of the room promptly ignoring him.

"We have a new comfortable recliner, so no need to bring up that excuse," Luke said eyeing him. "I'll run over and get your medication."

"I've got some with me, in the truck." Truth be told he'd been hoping they'd invite him to stay. He was stiff from the uncomfortable hospital chairs and needed to stretch out for a bit.

Once the house became quiet, Taylor considered going to Allison's bedroom to talk with her but then decided against it. The last thing he needed was to face-plant and cause a racket in the middle of the night.

Besides, everyone needed their rest. Especially Allison.

THE BRIGHTNESS OF the sunlight confirmed she'd slept in. Allison winced when she touched her forehead. Yep the accident had actually happened. One leg and then the other, she moved them and was glad there wasn't any discomfort. The same went for her arms and midsection, which she touched gingerly at first.

There was one last test. She wiggled her nose. "Ouch." Face and head were another matter. At least her headache was gone. Leah had checked on her several times during the night. Every two hours as the doctor had prescribed even after she grumbled and told her not too.

The mirror over the dresser beckoned from across the room. If she looked like a raccoon, it would be horrible for business. There was only so much makeup could do.

She slid from the bed and made her way to the mirror, unsure of what she'd seen. It turned out to be not as bad as she expected. However, it did look as if she'd been in a three-round fight with a boxer, who'd knocked her out with one punch to the nose.

"Shit."

Someone rapped at the door. Leah was persistent. She gave her that.

"Come in."

"Good morning." The first thing Taylor did was look her up and down. The only thing she wore was a tank and panties. "How are you feeling?"

Frozen to the spot, she could only gape at him. Her hair was probably all over the place. She had black eyes, a swollen nose and lip, and was half naked. "Uh...okay."

"Aren't you cold?" The corner of his lips twitched. He was looking at her nipples. The man ignored the fact she looked like Frankenstein's little sister to focus on her boobs.

Crossing her arms, she rushed to grab a robe Leah had thrown over the edge of the bed and put it on.

And queue the awkward silence. "Where are Luke and Leah?"

"Luke's out working. Leah went to town. Asked me to keep an eye on you." Once again he seemed to struggle to keep from a smirk. Taylor was enjoying this way too much.

"I'm fine. As soon as I get dressed, I am going to head to town. Need to work."

He stood without a cane, self-assuredness emanating from his large body. Want came next, like a wave over her. There was something about a man who radiated masculinity despite being injured. Even in his pain, which she knew he'd suffered for many months, he somehow maintained an outward appearance that he could kick anyone's ass without much trouble.

"You coming to the kitchen? Or should I come in?"

"What?" What was he up to? "I'll come to the kitchen. Give me a moment."

"Seem steady enough. Not that I could be much help. We'd probably land on the floor on top of each other." Again, the telltale smirk told her what he thought of them on the floor.

"Yeah, well I can manage. Good thing I don't need my face to walk."

The hazel gaze scanned her face. "Even with the bruising, you're beautiful."

Okay now she was blushing like an idiot. "Ha. You're funny."

I took several minutes to pull her hair into a messy bun, and then she splashed cold water on her face. There was some lip balm, face powder and a trial size tube of mascara in her purse. She used the lip balm and a bit of powder. Deciding the mascara would not help her eyes, she put it back into the makeup pouch.

Thankfully Leah had left behind sweatpants and a loose-fitting fleece long-sleeved shirt for her. After dressing, she felt much better.

Taylor was at the stove. The smell of bacon frying made her stomach tighten in anticipation.

She made toast and poured coffee, the morning ritual was like that of two people comfortable in each other's presence. The opposite was true. Tension was tangible as they managed to keep from getting too close to one another. Taylor limped a bit, but it wasn't as bad as she'd expected after the extensive surgery he'd undergone.

"How's your pain?"

He shrugged. "Barely there actually. I may keep the limp as a souvenir though. They want me to start walking without a cane. We'll see how that goes."

One plate in each hand, she went to the kitchen table and placed them down and then did the same with their coffee cups.

"I want to ask you something," she said once he sat across from her. "What is your friend Felicia's deal?"

Searching her face, brows came together in thought, Taylor let out a breath. "She's a good friend. We were partners. Why?"

Not sure how much to tell him, Allison wanted to kick herself for bringing the subject up. "She seemed a bit annoyed with me at the cookout the other night. Strange since I'd never met her." It was best not to say anything about the subsequent visit.

"Not sure. She can come across that way. But she's a good person."

She dipped a piece of toast into her egg yolk. Felicia was up to something and there wasn't any doubt in Allison's mind that for whatever reason Felicia didn't like her. Since Taylor was the only thing they had in common, it had to be the woman was infatuated with him.

"Maybe she is in love with you and thinks that for some reason you and I..." She waved between them. "Not sure how since I had a date with Ben."

"Or it could be she's interested in Ben." Taylor gave her a pointed look. "I'm sure Felicia is not interested in a relationship with me."

"Men can be clueless," Allison said lifting both shoulders. "Anyway. Are you going to town? I need a ride."

"I can do that." He pushed himself up and limped to the back door and opened it to let Luke and Leah's dogs out.

She followed his broad back from the doorway out. Both hands on the flat surface of the deck railing, he looked toward the horizon. From his wide shoulders to tapered waist, the man was a vision. However, he was also closed up and a mystery to Allison.

His mixed signals drove her crazy. He'd kissed her and acted as if he had more to say. Today, there was a wall ensuring she kept her distance. Allison had been sure he'd bring up the conversation they'd started the night before.

What was next? Was he interested in her or not? Did she even want to go out with him again? If he was the sleep with you and disappear type, it was best she continue on her plan to move on.

She went to the bedroom to put on her shoes and grab her things, hoping Leah would show up because she needed to get away from him as soon as possible.

Back in the living room, the dogs raced to her when she returned. After taking time to pet each one, she straightened and met Taylor's gaze. "Okay, I'm ready."

He stood and reached for the cane. "Let's do this." He limped to the door and did well using the cane only to go down the three steps. Although he concentrated on each movement, he also kept an eye on her. Allison opened the passenger truck door and climbed in. She'd considered opening his, but decided against it. He was trying to do for himself.

When he climbed in next to her after throwing the cane behind the seats, he huffed. "I could've fallen out there by myself. I'm going to tell Luke, you didn't watch me." He shook his head in mock displeasure.

"Ha." Allison rolled her eyes. This was the Taylor she liked, the easygoing one that enjoyed kidding and picking on people. Perhaps if she could change how she felt about him, they could remain friends and hang out.

And who was she kidding with that one?

CHAPTER TWENTY

T HINGS WERE ALWAYS quiet in the interlude between lunch and closing. Mindy stayed open until four most days, allowing for people to stop by for coffee after concluding whatever they did in town. Her employee usually left by two, leaving her alone the last couple of hours when she only served pastries, coffee and tea.

The kitchen was pristine, the floors swept and the counters wiped. There was little left to do but wait for customers and ensure the coffee was fresh.

She opened a drawer to get her phone and saw a handwritten note she'd shoved in there one day without much thought. The note was from Bryan. He'd tucked it into her purse and she'd found it one day after they'd argued over him doing something besides sitting at home all day.

It was an apology. A promise he'd move out soon, thanking her for all she did for him.

A huge lump formed as she swallowed and looked toward the door. Tears threatened. If only she'd taken the time to sit down and talk with her brother, done something more than be annoyed with him. Although she'd suspected he was in trouble, she'd not pushed to talk to the police. If nothing else, she should have told someone. But fear had kept her silent. Fear he was wanted and they'd put him in prison.

Being incarcerated would have been a better option than ending up dead in a dark street.

A sob wrenched out of her throat and Mindy squeezed her eyes shut, her fingers rubbing over the tattered piece of paper. When she opened them, Eric came into view just before the bells over the door announced he'd entered.

His dark gaze moved from her to the note. "What happened?" He was immediately around the counter with both hands on her shoulders. "Did someone threaten you?"

The police officer in him made Mindy relax, allowing the sorrow to dissipate for the moment to be replaced with awareness of how good it felt to be held.

"I could have done something. Should've called you...said something. I knew he was hiding details from me. Damn it." Mindy swallowed to keep from crying, but angry tears trailed down her cheeks. "Why didn't I? He could be alive right now."

Eric pulled her into an embrace and although his vest was hard and there was the crackling of the radio on his shoulder, she could not wish for a more comfortable harbor. Even if he'd always made her nervous and uncomfortable, there was no one she wanted there at the moment more than Eric.

After being so distant and frankly unfriendly to him, it was hard to move away from him at this moment. For a few minutes, she'd allow the closeness.

Any thought of a relationship made her nervous and Mindy didn't feel confident in her ability to chose a good man.

Even after her last relationship had turned physically abusive, she'd remained in it. It took a late-night visit to the emergency room before she found the strength to end it.

After starting over in Laurel Creek, she'd not been remotely interested in dating. Then one day Eric Hamilton had walked into the café. Their eyes had met and she'd felt something. Lightness in her spirit that had not been there for a long time, made its appearance.

When the butterflies showed up on his subsequent visits, it was time to panic. He could very well be the one person she could fall in love with and risk being hurt again.

"It's called survivor's remorse," Eric spoke softly into her ear, his hand brushing down her arm. "It's normal. However, know this." Finger's under her chin, he lifted her face. "The guy who was after him wouldn't have stopped until killing him. There was little you or anyone could have done."

"I don't understand. It didn't get him the drugs or money back."

Eric nodded. "I know, but it sends a clear message to others." He hugged her again. "You going to be okay?"

Mindy searched her mind to find what to say, but instead she couldn't stop looking into Eric's light colored eyes and as if hypnotized, her entire body went slack. She relaxed into his hold and was not at all reluctant when his mouth covered hers.

There was a sound in the kitchen, some sort of ding, and she pushed away from him. "I better check on the muffins. Help yourself to coffee... Thank you." She dashed into the kitchen and leaned against the wall just inside the doorway.

When the bell over the door sounded signifying he left or someone else came in, Mindy let out a breath. It was safe to come back out. There were no muffins in the oven. The bell was the end of the dishwashing cycle.

The café was empty. Eric stood outside speaking to a man. Once they finished, the man came inside and Eric met her gaze through the door.

His lips curved as he mouthed, "You're welcome."

CHAPTER TWENTY-ONE

"**W**HAT HAPPENED?" TORI stared at Allison, eyes wide. "Please tell me you weren't attacked."

So much for wearing concealer and makeup. "No, I hit a tree night before last. The airbag smashed my face. My car is totaled but the tree and whatever animal ran across the road are both good."

"Oh goodness." Her friend placed the box of vases she'd carried into the flower shop on the counter. "I hit a pole once. Messed my car up, but I pretended it was Tobias and felt better." Tori laughed at her own joke.

Allison grinned. "I wish you two would sit down and talk like adults instead of always arguing. There's something still there, you know?"

"Yep." Tori nodded with furrowed brows. "Mutual dislike."

The wreath on her decorating table in hues of gold and dark brown was finished and Allison walked around the counter to hang it on the front door. Soon they'd decorate for winter, but she held on to the fall décor as it was her favorite season, the changes in the air and colors made for a beautiful time of year in Montana.

"You know you don't dislike him. If he didn't argue with you regularly, you'd miss him."

Tori opened the door to the chiller where the flowers were stored. "Oh man, I know I said just greenery and baby's breath, but I think I want those pretty orange flowers too.

"Good choice, dahlias will last a good bit." Allison studied the short white vases. "Why don't you live dangerously and we use rosemary sprigs instead of the baby's breath?"

After Tori left, Allison was glad for the busy work. She clipped the ends of the flowers and lined them up. Two for each of the fourteen vases along with sprigs of rosemary and a green bud for additional color would make pretty table adornments. She pulled a spool of gold ribbon and tied a bow around each vase and then placed a piece of wet foam into the bottom of each.

She fussed more than necessary over each arrangement while drinking tea and listening to soft music. The fragrance of the flowers and her tea always filled her with calmness. And yet her mind kept wandering to what happened between her and Taylor nights earlier.

He'd kissed her and been so complimentary. If only he would be clear and tell her exactly what was going on.

Then again, she could have been direct and asked. After all, hadn't she once told Leah to take charge and go after what she wanted?

In all honestly, she wanted Taylor, and a relationship with him. One thing that had always annoyed her was how women sat around waiting for a guy to declare himself. Everyone knew men rarely thought further than the next time they'd get laid.

When it came to finances, careers and such, males were right on for the most part. But in her experience, they ended up in relationships without even knowing it.

Her lips curved. Perhaps it was time to take control.

Taylor answered on the second ring. His deep voice instantly sent a chill through her. "Hey, you all right?"

"Yes. I'm good. How are you?" Okay lame start, not sexy at all.

"Good." Pause.

Time to get a bit edgy. "Been thinking' about you."

"Oh yeah?" She hoped he was smiling. It sounded like he was. "About me?"

"The kiss mostly. You naked a lot." Whoa, she could barely keep from bursting out laughing. She sounded like a porn site.

"Augh. Wow. Was this last night after too much wine?" His voice got deeper. Then he cleared his throat. "I like the thought of you naked. Kinda early for phone sex, but I'm down."

Phone sex? No. No. No. This was going all wrong. Shit.

Allison tried again. "Would you like to come over for dinner?" Now it sounded like a booty call. This was not at all what she wanted. She'd wanted to let him know...

"I would, but I don't think I can manage your stairs yet. Can't manage a lot right now...unfortunately."

"Oh. Right. No. Damn it."

"Hey," he said quickly as if hoping she'd not hang up. "How about you come here? I can cook something. I'll get rid of Eric."

Allison burst out laughing. "I'm a dork. I didn't mean to call and start phone sex. I wanted to invite you for dinner to talk. That's it. I promise."

"I like that you think of me naked. So don't take that back." Taylor chuckled. "Come over tonight."

"Okay."

"Okay."

She hung up and groaned. What the hell had just happened? Question number two, how the hell was she supposed to get there? Her car was in some junkyard and other than a bicycle, which had a flat tire she had no transportation.

AN HOUR LATER, the aroma of Italian spices made her stomach grumble as she walked into Tori's restaurant. It was a small place but the food was amazing. Every night, the tables were filled with people wanting to sample the small menu of pasta, pizza and amazing Panini's.

Tori walked out wiping her hands on a dishtowel. "Let me help."

They walked back outside to a rolling cart that she'd used to bring the vases across the street on. Allison hadn't wanted to roll it inside since the sidewalk was wet from a slight drizzle.

"Can I borrow your car tonight?" Allison blurted as both walked in with a vase in each hand. "Taylor invited me over for dinner."

"Oooh." Tori wiggled her eyebrows. "He's ready to test drive the new hip huh?"

"No! It's not like that. Not at all."

"Don't worry about bringing my car back until tomorrow, I'm not going anywhere." Tori smiled.

After several more trips, they went about placing the flowers on each table.

LIGHTS SHINED OUT from the windows and two lampposts in front of Eric's house made it easy to see. The only vehicle was Taylor's truck, which was parked parallel to the porch. It was a good idea, to make it easier for him to get in and out without much trouble.

In jeans and a loose sweatshirt, she did her best not to dress for a booty call. Hopefully he'd get the message of her just wanting to talk.

Thankfully the application of full coverage makeup made her look less like an abuse victim and the knot on her forehead had lessened dramatically.

In her leather tote, she'd brought a bottle of wine although she remembered he'd not had anything to drink at the cookout due to medications. She'd need at least one glass to come up with the courage to tackle the conversation after the phone call.

"Come in," Taylor called out and she opened the door, which was unlocked.

Eric's house was what she expected from a bachelor's place. The only furnishings were a leather couch, a recliner and a huge television. Beside the television there was a gaming system on the entertainment unit and controllers of all kinds on the side tables.

The television was set to some sort of football talk show at a soft volume, with two wide shouldered men looking quite serious as they discussed the sport.

"I'm in here," Taylor called from the kitchen. "Sorry not to greet you, but didn't want this sauce to get lumpy."

Standing at the stove, he turned and smiled at her, a subtle dimple forming in his left cheek. "Hi."

"Hi." Allison dragged her gaze from his to notice he'd made a salad and placed a bottle of wine in an ice-filled caddy. "I brought wine too. Red."

"Making Alfredo sauce. Hope you like chicken Alfredo." He stirred the sauce and poured some sort of cream into it.

The aroma made her stomach growl. "It smells amazing." She went around the counter. "Would you like some wine?"

"Sure," he replied not turning and still stirring. "Either one is fine."

She poured his wine into two glasses and sipped from

hers. It was a buttery pinot grigio. "Didn't take you for a wine drinker."

"Yep," he said turning to look at her. "I developed a taste for it in Billings. A pal of mine was always going to wineries and tastings. I tagged along for something to do and ended up enjoying them."

She handed him the other glass and he held it up for a toast. "To quick healing." His gaze swept over her face. "Looks like you're mending pretty quick."

"That and good makeup." Allison moved away, his attention made her want to reach out and touch and that would certainly send the opposite message.

DINNER WAS DELICIOUS. They sat across from each other at the kitchen table and drank another glass of wine with the meal.

She looked around the room. "What did you do with Eric? He could have stayed."

"He went over to Tobias'. They're gaming or something."

"I don't want to impose. We could have met for dinner."

"Last time we went out to dinner, some guy slipped you his phone number."

Interesting, he had noticed. Allison chuckled. "That's right. I forgot about that."

"So you never called him?"

"Nope."

His lips curved but he didn't say anything as he pushed up to collect the plates. Allison helped him rinse and place them in the sink. He insisted she leave everything else as is and they went into the living room.

Taylor moved with an assured fluidity that made one barely notice his limp. Perhaps it was the fact he had an amazing and distracting physique so Allison couldn't help but follow his every movement.

"Anything you want to watch?" Taylor held the remote control and pointed it to the television. "Movie?"

"It doesn't matter." Channels flicked and different shows popped onto the screen, both or one would say no and Taylor would flip to the next one. Finally both stopped and stared at the screen as a couple in the throws of sex was splayed across the screen. Taylor's Adam's apple bobbed and Allison cleared her throat. "Porn channel?"

The screen changed to an action flick and Taylor put the control down. "HBO. Same thing."

He leaned forward and pressed a kiss to her lips. The action broke the ice and at once Allison felt at ease. "You need to tell me what's up. Something's going on in that pretty head of yours."

How to start? "Yes. I suppose there is. I've decided to take my own advice and be up front with you."

"Okay." His face hardened as if he waited for her to tell him she was going to die or something. "What's up?"

After a couple sips of wine, she put the glass aside and she met his gaze. "I want to date. Get to know you on a personal level."

"Date?" Clue in the oblivious male. "Go out to places you mean? I though we already do that."

"No, we don't. We went out once as friends. You guarded me after the murder. We slept together and then you never called me again."

"You know why." Once again, he pressed a kiss to her lips. "I want to date you too."

"Taylor. Are you taking me serious?"

Another Kiss. "Very much so."

"Stop it." Her pulse was jumping and it became hard to breathe normally. "I mean a relationship."

His brows went from furrowing to rising. "You don't want that."

"Yes, I do." This time she couldn't help but kiss him back. "I want to see where we can take this. There's definitely chemistry between us."

With a long intake of breath, his wide chest lifted and lowered and he pulled Allison against him. The hard surface was warm and enticing her to press her lips against his throat.

"Not sure I can satisfy a woman right now Allison. It'll be a while before I can do much. You don't need to be dating a man who can't make love to you the right way."

She pushed up, resisting the urge to smack him. "Taylor, seriously? Although I admit sex with you is great, that is not my main motivator. I care for more than your body. Despite what I said during the stupid phone call earlier."

He didn't look convinced. Instead once again pulled her against him. This time Allison gave in to the urge and kissed his throat, trailing her lips from the side of his jawline to his ear. "You know you like me," she whispered and traced his ear with her tongue. "You wanna kiss me."

The deep rumble of his chuckle was oh so sexy.

Taylor turned his head to the side allowing her more access to his throat. She slid her right hand down his chest past the ridges of his stomach, careful to avoid his injured side.

A low rumble sounded when she traced the hardness between Taylor's legs and his mouth took hers. The kiss was hungry and hard, his need for more without question.

Taylor pulled back, his breathing shallow and fast. "How about a refill on that wine?"

There was no question in her mind he was attracted to her, but he'd not agreed to a relationship and without saying it out loud had turned down her offer.

How do you hide disappointment coupled with embarrassment? He was not interested in her outside of sex. The "at least you tried" self-talk would not work to help remove the sting of his rejection.

"No thank you. I better head back. Better take my time and not hit a tree with Tori's car."

His downcast gaze hid whatever he was thinking as Allison slid to stand. With the wine glasses in hand, she went to the kitchen to place them on the counter and retrieve her purse.

"Thank you for dinner Taylor. It was delicious."

Taylor stood by the door and when she reached for her jacket, which she'd thrown over the back of a chair, he covered her hand.

"I'm not sure I want you to leave."

What the hell was that supposed to mean? She was seriously starting to get tired of his mixed signals.

His nonverbal reply had basically been, "I can't make love to you, therefore nix on the relationship".

Followed by "I don't want you to leave, therefore, maybe there's a chance".

"What do you want? You confuse me."

Not taking his eyes from her, he slipped the purse strap from her shoulder and put it on the chair.

"Don't be confused." When Taylor took a step toward her, Allison took one back. Her back against the door, Taylor trapped her and took her chin in his hand to tip her face up. "I want more with you. I just don't want you to settle…" he left the rest of the sentence unsaid, as he searched her face.

There it was. Insecurity. The one thing she'd never think or expect when it came to Taylor Hamilton. He was always so strong. Like an unmovable boulder to which one could cling when the current of life threatened.

"Never settle Allison. You are so vibrant."

"Are you fucking kidding me right now?" Her voice

pitched up a couple of octaves. "One thing you are not is someone a woman "settles" for. Have you seen yourself in the mirror? I mean, yeah you're hot as all get out. But how shallow do you think I am?" She was rambling and needed to stop.

Thank goodness, he covered her mouth with his.

"Come back. Sit down," Taylor said.

"I can't. I better go." There was little certainty in her voice. Even she could hear the lack of commitment to leaving. But damn it, it was a mistake to stay there. Not only could things become awkward, but also he did not want a relationship. Taylor was being a nice guy and making sure they remained friendly.

"Maybe we can go out for pizza later this week," she offered. "I have to go to the city in a couple of days to get a car. Ben's taking me. He likes car shopping. Or so he says." Once again Allison couldn't stop talking. When nervous, her mouth went on automatic ramble mode. "Maybe I'll get a little truck this time…"

"Allison." His deep voice stopped her babbling and his hand cupping her face made her still. "I do want you. More than anything, but…"

"Stop it Taylor. Tell me what do you want? If you are willing to try a relationship, I am too. But if you're not sure then I'm gone. There won't be any hard feelings.

"I do want you…us… it's just that…" Taylor let out a long breath.

He stopped talking when Allison slipped her hands

under the dark t-shirt he wore. As the fabric rose, it revealed a toned taut muscular physique that only came from constant workouts.

She remained transfixed when his hazel eyes met hers and she unfastened the top button of his jeans. Once again uncertainty flickered, but only for a moment as the corner of his lips lifted.

"You sure you want to see this?"

Just above the waistband on his left side two scars peeked. The skin was pink seeming not yet totally healed.

"Yes." Allison nodded, more interested in the man than a scar. She understood how important it was for him. Men after all were visual in nature. He could reveal his intestines hanging out and it would not diminish her attraction. Okay so that was a bit gross.

For her, what was important was the strong heart beating in his chest and the soul of the man.

He lowered the left side and shame on her, but instead of looking at the scar, her eyes shot to the trail of dusting of hair that went down from his belly button.

Finally, she dragged her gaze from that point to where the laparoscope had dug into his body. Three deep circles puckered the skin in a large triangle through jagged scarred skin.

Fresh and older scars intermingled creating something like she'd seen on burn victims. Although not attractive in the least, it wasn't as bad as she'd imagined.

"Can I touch you?"

Taylor nodded and held his breath. "Yeah."

With tentative fingers, she brushed over the skin. It was warm, soft and not any different than normal skin, other than the dips and ridges."

When her hand slid over where the holes had been stitched, Taylor tensed. Allison pulled her hand back. "I'm sorry, did I hurt you?"

"No." He frowned. "It feels good actually. The itching is pretty bad."

He turned to his right so she could get a better look and the sight made her want to cry. Where the bullets exited they'd caused a lot of damage. The surgeons had pulled the skin tight to close up the wounds, which caused puckering and deformity. A patch of sorts had been added and still the skin tugged up from his hip to the side.

"They tried to fix it, but Eric said it looks worse."

Although he spoke in a casual tone, it was obvious by the hesitancy of each word, that he was nervous about her reaction. This time she didn't ask permission, and touched the skin. "I'm glad it's not as painful as it looks. I caught a glimpse of your back when you were at my place. I have to agree with Eric. Why did they go back in?"

His wide shoulders lifted and lowered. "My pain had gotten bad. The bones did not heal properly. They had to do some bone smoothing so while they were in there…" He let out a breath. "Doc said it would help with the tightness of the earlier surgery. It does feel better."

It was not just the scarring that caused Taylor to hesitate when it came to a relationship. Allison was sure something else happened. With most of the surgery concentrated on his hip, his movements were no doubt impeded.

Walking around so to stand before him, she smiled up at him. "You know there are many ways to be intimate. Whatever is going on right now…it won't stop me from wanting to be with you."

"I know. It's just that, eventually it will bother you."

"Is it not supposed to get better? Are we talking about your hip or something else?" It occurred to her that perhaps something had gone wrong during surgery and he'd been rendered without the ability to become erect. No that wasn't it. Just moments earlier on the couch…

His eyes grew round as he figured out where her thoughts went. "No. Yeah, I still can. Shit Allison, let's figure this out. Show me what you mean."

"What? Now? Here?"

"I'm being an idiot. I don't want to lose you." He took her hand and placed it just below the waistband of his pants. His top buttons were undone and there was an obvious bulge just below. "Show me."

And queue the fish out of water mouth opening and closing. Not only because of being caught off guard but the sudden faster heart beat.

Pulse racing, her breathing hitched and Allison couldn't wait to show him exactly what she'd been daydreaming of doing to him.

CHAPTER TWENTY-TWO

TAYLOR COULDN'T MOVE. Not only had he just uttered words that could not be taken back, but also he was pretty sure his legs would give out if he took a step.

Damn Allison was breathtaking. She'd done her best to tone down her appearance with a baggy sweatshirt and those jeans that hugged her curves just right. But the smolder in her eyes and the light pink of her lush lips sent every single ounce of blood within him to rush between his legs.

Hopefully he'd not make a fool of himself and drop his load in a minute flat. She cocked her head to the side in thought, her lips curving into a wicked smile.

"Come here." Taking his hand, she guided him to the couch. Once in front of it, her half-closed eyes moved from his mouth down the length of his torso to his pants. She pushed gently on his hurt side and then on the right until his pants were down to his knees.

Taylor helped her out and pushed them off with his

feet. And, there he stood in boxer briefs, erection so hard it pushed out the flimsy fabric announcing there was little more she had to do to excite him.

"Wow," she whispered and didn't that just make him want to crow like a fucking rooster.

Guiding him to lay back on the cushions, Taylor allowed it, more than happy to give her free reign over his body.

With one foot on the floor, his left side and stretched out leg were cushioned against the plush leather of the couch. His already fast breathing spiked when she loomed over him and pulled off the now offensive hoodie. Beneath it she wore a flimsy excuse for a tank top and no bra to constrict her full breasts. She slipped out of the jeans and wearing satiny blue panties and matching tank, she straddled him just below the hips.

Her lips curved when he reached for her. "Come here. I want your mouth on mine." Allison complied and he took full advantage. Kissing her and driving his tongue between her lips while running his hands all over her satiny bare skin.

ALLISON WASN'T QUITE sure what was about to happen. Here she was prepared to make love with Taylor and without a clue what would or wouldn't hurt him.

The time he took devouring her mouth as if starved gave her a feel for how strong he was. She'd straddled him, being careful to keep her weight on her legs and not on his injured hip. Yet when he pulled her against him, the fact didn't seem to bother him. Excitement and adrenaline had a way of numbing pain, so she'd not been swayed by his actions as much. Men would go to extraordinary lengths to cover up their weaknesses.

No matter that he'd undressed and shown her his battered body, Taylor was a proud strong man, not used to vulnerabilities. Once again lifting just enough to not put her whole weight on him, she looked down at Taylor.

With half closed eyes and a devilish grin, he lifted a brow. "I believe you were going to show me something?"

Of course, she was. If Allison had her way, she'd dive straight down and take him into her mouth. But the buildup would be what made the whole thing worth it. Not just for him, but for her as well.

Already her breathing was labored. The rapid succession of her heart's beats seemed to match Taylor's pulse when she pressed her lips to the side of his neck. She'd found his erogenous zone. The spot just below his ear brought happy grunts.

The sexy sounds erupted and she lingered at the spot, licking in a circular motion before nipping the tender skin, just enough to let him feel it.

His body was enticing in a way only a man's could be. He was all male; hard, and muscular with peaks and valleys in just the right places. She ran her hands down his pectorals, enjoying the feathering of hair down the center.

Allison hadn't been with many men, but she was experienced enough to know this was a time to slow down and savor. Literally.

"Hey." His piercing hazel gaze swept over her. "Take off that top."

Unable to keep from it, her lips curved and she straightened. It was nice to be admired so openly. As if in a trance, Taylor remained still. Watching, his gaze following her hands as she lifted the tank up her sides and over her head.

HER PULSE ACCELERATED when he reached out to cup her breasts. "Damn, you are so fucking beautiful."

Of course she didn't believe him. In a strange way, Allison wanted him not to admire her so much, while at the same time hoped he'd continue to lavish her with praise. Talk about confused.

Pushing her shoulders back, she allowed her head to fall back and she closed her eyes.

"Oh." Allison's breath caught when he circled her nipples with the pads of his thumbs. Sweet heat raced from every extremity sending waves of need.

Each movement was slow and measured. Both were uncertain of which path to take, but also determined to continue forth.

Good. It felt so good. Each touch, breath and kiss just enough and yet leaving her wanting more.

Taylor glided his palms down her sides and Allison

took the opportunity to move down. She licked a path down the center of his chest, trailing her palms behind. With her mouth, she pushed the waistband of his boxer-briefs aside, while gently tugging them down far enough to free his erection.

His stomach sunk when he inhaled sharply. Taylor had not expected this. By the way he trembled, the excitement that he felt was accompanied by apprehension.

Taking his hardness in hand, Allison looked up to meet his gaze and licked her bottom lip. It was gratifying when his lips curved in response.

Gently, she trailed the fingers of her right hand across the edges of his scarring. "Is it tender here?"

"Ugh...no...a little," he finally admitted.

"Okay. I will make sure to avoid that area." She kept her voice soft and husky. The tone not really made up, but more a result of the fire burning within.

Unable to keep from it, Allison laved the underside of his erection. From base to tip, she licked every inch, loving the subtle saltiness. After doing it twice, she took the tip and sucked it into her mouth.

"Fuck," Taylor murmured, and his hips jutted up just a bit. "That feels amazing."

She took him in and pressed her tongue against the silky underneath while taking him in deeper.

With each stroke Allison took more of him into her mouth until he hit the back of her relaxed throat. She wanted to go harder, faster, but held back.

It was so different with him right now. Without any kind of persuasion, he did indeed move her to do more, to be open. Brazen. Maybe that was the word for it. Allison wanted to experiment, to try new things. Pictures of their naked bodies intertwined formed, sending her already hot body into a furnace of desire and want.

Taylor's fingers weaved through her curls as she sucked harder and harder, taking more and more of him. Slurps and soft gagging noises filled the room, as she couldn't stop herself. She needed to finish him off, to taste his release.

"Shit," Taylor gritted the word out, his entire body tensing. "I'm gonna come. You might want to move."

Instead of doing what he said, Allison continued the assault. Her cupped hand trailing behind while the other caressed his sac. To have someone so strong undone by her was a high she wasn't ready to give up.

"Ah!" Taylor came with force. His muscular body tensed and a hoarse cry filled the room as Allison continued licking and sucking to ensure he was completely and utterly satisfied.

Finally, he went limp, his broad chest lifting and lowering with each hurried breath. Allison wiped her mouth on his thigh. What would happen next? She needed her own release. Perhaps it was time to put her money where her mind had gone just moments earlier.

"Come here," Taylor instructed. He tugged her none too gently up past his chest to once again lay over him. "Let me take care of you."

It didn't take long. Within ten minutes, Allison was thrashing and screaming while Taylor's hot mouth worked her sex, his fingers slipping in and out of her.

CHAPTER TWENTY-THREE

TORI GRINNED WHEN opening the door to find a half-dazed Allison. "Sorry I'm so late returning the car."

"No worries girl. Hope you had fun."

"Umm hmm." Allison didn't look her in the eye, but instead held out the keys. "I filled it up."

Moving aside, she gestured for Allison to come inside. "Wanna come in and have a glass of wine?"

The only light in her living room came from the television. She'd been watching a superhero show and it was on pause. "We can stare at Captain America."

Allison shook her head. "No thanks. I better get home. Going to Billings early in the morning to look at cars."

"Okay I'll watch you from here." Tori walked to the edge of her small yard to keep an eye on Allison until the lights came on upstairs.

By the sheen in her friend's eyes, she held back a steamy secret. Tori chuckled as she settled back into the couch. She'd give her a day, then armed with wine and chocolate, every single detail would be coaxed out.

Her cell buzzed. It was certainly a busy time for it being almost eleven at night.

"Hello." Tori's eyes widened when Captain America's broad chest filled the screen. Not wanting another distraction by the form of her mother or sister calling, once again, she paused the movie.

"Hello?"

"Hey. You talk to my brother?"

Tobias. Great. Tori scowled at the phone. "What the hell are you talking about Tobias?"

There was a stretch of silence. The sound of shuffling came next. Afterwards it was as if bedding moved and then a clearing of the throat.

"I didn't mean to call you. Thought I called my sister."

Right. The man was usually pretty creative in finding ways to antagonize her. This one was pretty lame.

"Whatever." She wanted to hang up, but curiosity got the best of her. "Is something wrong with Luke?"

"Like you give a damn."

Her eyes narrowed. "About Luke, yes I do. About Taylor too. You on the other hand, not so much."

"Good thing the feeling is mutual." Tobias didn't hang up. She could hear his breathing.

Tori's finger hovered over the red button on the screen. "Are you going to answer my question?"

"Luke's okay. He had a small episode, but Leah

helped him through it. My sister found out some information about a center that is getting good results from a treatment they're doing."

Although she didn't care much for Tobias, at one time she would have died for him. Luke on the other hand, had always been distant and reserved. Now since returning from several tours to war zones, he'd developed into an outright intimidating man.

The hulking muscular handsome Luke had been through hell and survived. Every inch of him exuded a silent "barely there" restraint.

"Ok. Glad to hear it."

"Yeah, whatever." Taylor said something else, but Tori didn't hear it. She'd moved the phone away from her ear.

"Kiss my ass," she called out and this time Tori did hang up. It was best to do so than to try and have any kind of civil conversation with Tobias.

Yes, she was aware she'd been a bitch when she'd broken it off years ago. Although just a teenager, even then, she should have had more decency than to break up with her fiancé the way she'd done it. At this point, it was water under the bridge, for her at least. Hell, twenty years had passed since the breakup. And both had been married and divorced in the time since. One would think a person would have dropped the resentment issue.

For Tobias, the entire situation seemed to grow worse with each passing year. It was almost as if he resented her more and more. Some days she considered that perhaps it would be best to move away. The blame was hers after all. All of it.

Tori never tried to attack Tobias on that front. However, they'd moved past that point a long time ago. Tobias latest tactic was to pick fights with her on any topic. Leah had once kidded that the constant bickering had turned into a sort of love-language between them.

The only thing between her and Tobias was animosity. That her stomach tumbled at seeing him was never because of attraction anymore. No, what she felt was dread at whatever brought him around and what he'd say or do that would anger her to the point of wanting to lash out physically.

SO MUCH FOR the next day starting out well. Rain pelted at her bedroom window and while Tori showered and got dressed, an employee called in sick. Something about cooler weather and rain. It made people want to stay home. Hell, she wanted to stay home.

Good thing she loved her job. Owning Victoria's had been a dream come true and Tori did enjoy it most days.

To put the cherry on top of her craptastic morning however, Tobias' truck was parked just down the block. She would have to walk past it to get to the restaurant.

Umbrella up, she rushed across the street to avoid running into Tobias. A woman stood under an awning and waved to her. It was an older woman, Ellen, the owner of a small bookstore one street over. "Hey Tori.

You won't believe this…"

What Tori couldn't believe was that the woman wanted to have a conversation in the pouring rain. She hesitated when Ellen, who'd pulled her hood up, hurried toward her. "My tire is flatter than a pancake and I have to visit my husband at the senior center today."

Tori craned her neck to see a man was crouched down replacing the tire. "You actually got someone to come out and change it? I would have loaned you my car."

"Oh honey." Ellen patted her shoulder. "Sweet Tobias offered to change it. He would have taken me, but said he's got someone coming to town today."

Sweet Tobias? Right. Tori looked again and sure enough it was him. The man was drenched, but didn't seem to mind by the grin when he looked to Ellen. "All done Mrs. Dean."

Once again Ellen patted Tori. "It's a shame. You let a good one go. I bet his sweetie will start pressuring him for a ring soon."

Sweetie? Tori blew out a breath and rolled her eyes at the retreating woman's back. Whoever the "sweetie" was, she could have all of "sweet Tobias".

"Hey," Tobias called. "You don't have to rush. You won't melt that's for sure."

Not wanting to scream out an obscenity, Tori mouthed "Fuck You," and flashed him the middle finger.

CHAPTER TWENTY-FOUR

A LL HOSPITALS SMELLED the same. Sickness had a
very specific smell. It lingered in the cold air-
conditioned air coating everything. The hallway to the
room was long, but it was easy to see which room Felicia
was in. Cops stood just outside the door refusing to
leave. By the shadows under the eyes of the first one
Taylor approached, they'd been there since the night
before.

Three officers had been shot. One had died. Felicia
lingered, one foot barely on the right side of living.
Recognition flickered in the tired officer's gaze. "They're
not letting anyone in right now. A doctor and a couple of
nurses just rushed in. The machines were all bleeping."

Taylor moved around him and peered through the
glass into what looked to be controlled chaos. A man in a
long white coat stood over the bed. With one hand he
pressed a stethoscope against Felicia's chest and everyone
looked to a monitor. The doctor barked out an order and
made sweeping motions to a nurse. Still talking and

directing, he then reached for a long syringe that the nurse held out.

It was obvious to Taylor they were attempting to restart Felicia's heart. His hands curled into fists as adrenaline rushed over him. He wanted to rush in and scream into her ear, tell her to fight. She'd beaten the odds before. There was no reason this time it had to be different.

He both struggled to breathe and then held his breath unable to take his eyes from the doctor's face. The doctor's expression was schooled, unreadable as the man stared at the monitor and once again pressed his stethoscope to Felicia's chest.

The man's brow crinkled and he said something to the nurses. One of them looked toward the glass meeting Taylor's gaze. The older woman was obviously experienced because he couldn't read anything in her expression either.

Once again the doctor said something and all three seemed to relax. Their shoulders fell, it was then Taylor knew.

Placing his stethoscope around his neck, the doctor walked toward the door. Before he reached it a man pushed Taylor aside and walked into the room.

"You get back there and keep trying." The hoarseness in the man's tone made Taylor take notice. It was then he recognized him as John Morris, Captain at the Billings Police Department.

"Don't give up doc," Morris pointed toward the bed.

"She's one of my best."

The doctor was a tall man, youthful and attractive. The only indication he was older where the strands of silver through his dark brown hair.

"I'm sorry Captain Morris. She's gone." He stood his ground, not backing up when Morris walked up almost touching him. "We did what we could. Her internal organs, the major ones were all shot."

From what Taylor had heard, drug dealers with semi-automatic rifles had opened fired when Felicia and her partner had responded to a domestic abuse situation unaware it was a meth house.

By the time back up arrived, Felicia and her partner had both been fatally injured.

"No," Taylor walked past the men to where Felicia lay surrounded by now silent equipment, lines still attached to her.

Her face was perfect, no bruising or any kind of injury that he could see above the shoulders. It was as if she was sleeping.

There was a scream and Felicia's mother raced to the door, her face transformed with emotion as her husband tried to hold her back. The doctor went to them and began explaining what he'd already said to the Captain.

Taylor stumbled backward to give her family room to stand next to where the ashen face Morris stood transfixed, his gaze locked to the bed.

A low hum sounded, at first Taylor looked around the room to locate where it originated. It grew louder. It was then he realized it came from his head. Lights swam before his eyes and he took a deep breath.

It was not like before when he'd been in and out of consciousness not knowing if he'd walk again. His career had ended in that same hospital, but he'd survived.

Felicia had made it too. That time. Why not now? He must have made a sound because one of the nurses came over to him and touched his shoulder. "I think you need to sit down."

Afraid he'd pass out, Taylor allowed the woman to guide him to a chair. Nothing like being a pansy-ass at a time like this. But he'd rather be a sitting idiot than one passed out on the floor.

"Hamilton, right?" Felicia's father stood beside the bed, his hand on his wife's shoulder.

"Yes sir," Taylor willed himself to stand and unsteadily made it to where the man stood and held out his hand. "I came as soon as I heard."

"Thank you." The man's gaze moved to Taylor's left side. "She told me you were having surgery again." The man struggled to swallow. "Felicia cared a great deal for you. She said you were her best friend."

Taylor squeezed his eyes shut and looked to the floor fighting back against the tidal wave of pain. They'd been partners, at one time lovers, but through it all, she was right. They'd been close friends.

A heavy palm weighed on his right shoulder as whoever approached from behind offered support. Taylor could not move. He willed time backward, to the last time he'd seen Felicia. She'd walked into Eric's house the night of the cookout to annoy him, talking loudly and commenting about the football game.

Although Felicia was young, mid-thirties, she'd seen more than her share of things. She had been an experienced cop who would have gotten far in the force.

Now her time had come and Taylor refused to believe it. He stared at the woman on the bed.

Wake up. Stop it already Felicia. It's not your time. Wake the fuck up.

When she didn't move, not listening to him as usual, Taylor turned on his heel and walked out. He kept moving until ending up outside the hospital. The area, which looked to be a break area thankfully, was deserted. Taylor could not breathe, his throat to thick to allow him air to pass. A sound akin to a sob erupted and he fell more than sat onto a hard bench.

Not able to keep from it, he rested his elbows on his knees, covered his face and cried.

CHAPTER TWENTY-FIVE

S OMEONE WAS THERE. Allison wasn't sure what woke her, but whatever it was had her instantly wide-awake. She sat up in the bed and craned her neck listening intently.

Knocks? Yes, there were three knocks followed by another three. She slipped from the bed to look out of the window. A truck was parked on the street. It looked to be the same model as either Taylor's or Tobias'.

Jerking on her robe, she went downstairs and upon seeing the expression instantly went into panic mode. Something about the hollowness in Taylor's eyes made her stomach sink. Whatever brought him there so late, or early as it was, had to be bad.

Allison jerked the door open and stepped back. As soon as he walked through the door, she threw her arms around him. Taylor held her tight, his face buried in her hair.

"What happened?" She finally managed while hoping he'd not say.

He didn't speak, instead moved back and reached to close the door. "I'm sorry to come here so late. I need to crash for a couple hours. Is that okay?"

"Yes. Of course. Did you and Eric have a fight or something?"

Searching her face as if not understanding her question, Taylor frowned.

Considering he seemed to be in some sort of haze, Allison took his hand. "Let's go upstairs, I'll help you. Would you like a drink?"

"Yeah. That would be good."

In silence, he watched her, not speaking while she poured port into two small glasses. "Sorry, it's the strongest thing I have."

He eyed the glass and drank half of the contents. "It's good."

"Yeah, I buy it every year at a winery in Portland."

Shadows flickered in his gaze when he looked directly at her for the first time since arriving. "Felicia died today."

"Oh my God." Allison could feel her eyes grow wide. "What happened?"

"Domestic gone real bad. Both she and her partner were gunned down."

Allison's knees weakened. The woman was so full of life, so strong. When she'd come to warn her to treat Taylor right, she'd not pulled any punches. Even if Allison didn't particularly care for her, she'd respected Felicia's faithful friendship to Taylor and to her career.

She wrapped her arms around his shoulders and rested her head next to his. "I'm so sorry. So very sorry."

WHEN THE SUN rose, just a short time later, Taylor remained awake. He was exhausted, but his mind refused to shut down. Captain Morris had warned him off trying to do anything about the shooting.

The gunmen had been arrested and waited indictment. Investigators were at the scene ensuring every single item was not just collected, but also double-checked. They would ensure not one loophole would be available for any scumbag lawyer to use and potentially free the killers.

Taylor had gone over there after leaving the hospital. Out of respect for having been Felicia's partner, they'd allowed him free rein. That was until Morris arrived.

It didn't matter what the Captain instructed. He'd ensure the sons of bitches that killed her never got away with it. Not only would they serve time for the murders, but also he'd find as much dirt as possible on them. So much fucking dirt, they'd never know life outside of prison again.

Eyes like sandpaper, he limped to the window and blinked at the rising sun in the horizon.

Another day had begun. It was the first one without Felicia in it. She'd always said that when she kicked it, her funeral better be a good one. Although morbid, spending long hours together had meant they'd talked about a lot of stuff.

Though most of the other deputies considered Felicia hard, he'd known under her tough exterior was the heart of a lion and but also the softness of a woman who cared too much. It had been the reason for how their relationship had progressed. They'd both not known how to deal with being apart after the shooting and had used sex to connect.

Although it had been passionate, there had never been more than friendship and eventually they'd come to realize it. Now though he'd give anything to be back in the hotel room arguing with her about what an asshole he was.

There was shuffling in the other room. Allison had finally stopped trying to convince him to get some sleep and had gone to bed. Although originally he did plan to sleep, once he was alone, too many thoughts had invaded.

"Taylor?" She came from the bedroom and stopped at seeing him at the window. "Did you get any rest?"

Rest no. Sleep either. "Yeah some. Thanks."

By the lift of her right eyebrow and flat line of her lips, she didn't believe him. "I'm going to make eggs, bacon, and toast. You're going to eat and then sleep."

"I'll go home. Have to talk to Eric about some things. Then I'm going to be in Billings for a few days." He sat at the table knowing it was best to eat and give Eric time to get up. "I'm going to help with the investigation. There can't be one single mistake."

She must have seen the determination in his gaze because instead of saying anything, Allison nodded. Coffee was slid in front of him. The dark liquid swirled with the creamer.

"Would you like me to come with you?"

"What?" He wasn't sure what the proper response was and needed time to consider how best to deal with it. Of course, they'd decided to try and make a relationship between them work. Unfortunately at the moment, his brain vacated and he stared at Allison.

"I can come to Billings and be there for you."

"No. I'll be gone the entire time. There's nothing for you to do."

His answer was wrong. The gruffness in his voice left no doubt that he didn't want, nor need her there. In truth, he wasn't sure.

"Okay." Allison turned to the stove, her shoulders straight.

"Look I don't need this right now. I can't deal with you and what happened." Taylor stood. "I better go. Give me some time all right? My head is all over the place."

She whirled toward him, hurt radiating. "All I did was offer to come if you needed me too." Hands up, she blew out a breath. "Look just go. Don't worry about having to "deal" with me." With that, she stalked away to her bedroom slamming the door behind her.

Too tired, that was the problem. He'd taken it out on her and it wasn't fair. Taylor went to the stove and stirred the bacon. Moments later, he fried eggs and slipped them onto two plates as the toaster dinged and perfectly browned bread popped up.

Once everything along with short glasses filled with orange juice was on the table, he went to Allison's bedroom.

She'd not locked the door.

"I'm sorry. I don't know why I said that. I made breakfast." He took her by the shoulders and she shrugged him off. Taylor persisted, tipping up her face and wincing at the shiny tear-filled eyes.

"Don't cry Allison. I'm tired and upset. Saying stupid shit." He pressed a soft kiss to her lips. "I do need you. Need to know that when this is over, you will be here for me."

She sniffed. "I know you're going through a horrible time. I can't imagine. But don't push me away or snap at me. That's not fair."

Of course she was right. And he needed sleep. Time to regroup before going off and doing what Captain Morris warned him against.

"I need to talk this out. Tell me what you think," he said tugging her hand and leading his beautiful woman to the table.

Once she sat and he lowered to his seat, he began talking. By the time they'd finished their meal, not only did he have a plan, but could barely keep his eyes open.

"Take a nap. I'll wake you when Eric gets here." Allison pushed him toward the bedroom. He stretched out across the soft mattress on his stomach. The bedding smelled of her, some sort of flowery lemony scent that reminded him of her vibrant curls. Taylor fell asleep to the sounds of Allison cleaning up, soft music that she preferred playing in the background.

"YOU'RE TOO CLOSE to the case. It's a bad idea." Eric frowned into his coffee. "I don't think Morris will agree."

Taylor gave no shits. He'd either be added on to the investigation as a consultant, or he'd do it as a nosy civilian. It mattered little to him.

"I have to do this," Taylor responded looking over at Mindy, who kept sliding glances toward their table. "You ask her out yet?"

This time it was Eric who became animated. "I'm working up to it."

"Don't wait too long. I've seen Ben hovering the last couple of times I've been in here."

At the comment, Eric got to his feet and went to where a wide-eyed Mindy looked up at him. Taylor had lied about Ben and now he smiled as Eric said something to Mindy who nodded slowly.

Her lips curved and cheeks colored prettily, making Taylor wonder how long before they'd work up the courage to hold hands. Eric had always been shy, more of a book nerd than a dater during high school. He did have a steady girlfriend, but they'd broken up during their college years.

Although engaged once, his cousin didn't seem inclined to marry. Now as the guy neared forty, Taylor figured he might just be one of those guys that preferred life on his own.

Eric settled across from him. "Asked her over to watch a movie."

"Netflix and chill?" Taylor chuckled.

"What? Should I get Netflix? I was going to ask her what she wanted to see and rent the movie."

"Never mind."

"Come on man, tell me." Eric blew out a breath. "I'm outta practice with this dating shit."

"No. Way." Taylor said it as two separate words mimicking how Eric sometime spoke. "Nervous. Virgin."

"Shut. Up." Eric rolled his eyes. "Been awhile, that's all. Not sure how to go about things anymore."

Mindy had gone back into the kitchen and Taylor knew the woman was probably having some sort of giggle chat with her friend. "I'm sure she'll be fine with whatever you plan. Movie and a pizza are the perfect first date."

"Okay. Good." Eric let out a breath and his face transformed back to all cop. "If you're insisting on going to Billings, talk to Morris in a neutral environment. Meet him outside his office. From what you've told me, he's a good leader. He'll know you won't back down."

Not that he needed Eric's permission, but Taylor felt better at knowing his cousin backed him.

"One thing though," Eric said holding up a hand.

"The investigation comes first. If at anytime you feel like you're losing control, pull back or pull out. Better to not fuck things up. Whoever killed Felicia has to rot in jail."

CHAPTER TWENTY-SIX

A LLISON WOKE WITH a start. It had been almost a month, twenty-five days to be exact since Taylor left for Billings. From what she gleaned, he was hired on as a consultant for Felicia's case. Even though Eric had tried valiantly to talk him out of it, Taylor had remained steadfast.

Eventually, Eric had admitted to Allison that any cop of honor would do exactly what Taylor did. Demand to be part of the investigation that killed his or her partner.

And although it made sense to her on one level, a part of her worried that she'd be competing with a dead woman if her relationship with Taylor continued.

So far he'd given no indication to worry her. Well other than being in Billings. He called her nightly and had come back to Laurel Creek at least once a week. She'd not offered to go to Billings, not after the way he'd reacted, but it didn't mean she didn't hope he'd ask her to.

Now they were to spend a couple of days together.

He'd called the night before to ask if she could take time off so they could go away together. The offer had both baffled and excited her.

His hip had gotten progressively better and making love didn't take so much creativity, per se. Admittedly, they'd kept it a bit on the wild side. Thanks to having to be careful, they'd found it fun and exciting to try new things. For the first time in her life, Allison was able to experiment and try new things with a lover.

Albeit, they'd ended up in fits of laughter when something they tried failed. The moment lost, they'd sat up in bed and talked. Sometimes had meandered to the kitchen in the middle of the night for an impromptu meal.

Their relationship was fresh and still new. She'd finally mentioned it to Jaden, who'd been very receptive to the idea of meeting Taylor.

Now as she pondered what would happen during their weekend away, she bit her bottom lip in anticipation.

The bell over the door jingled and Allison lifted her head to see the last person she expected to walk through the door.

David, her ex-boyfriend smiled wide, and opened his arms as if she'd be so relieved to see him that she'd throw herself against him.

"Hi," she said and walked toward him. The hug was too tight for her liking, but she allowed it.

"God I've missed you," he said pushing back his

glasses while giving her a once over. "You look great."

"Thanks." Allison pushed a curl behind her ear. "What brings you to Laurel Creek?" Dumb question as he'd just proclaimed to miss her. But she hoped he'd not say her nonetheless.

"Don't be silly. I had to see you." He reached for her and she pretended not to notice while moving away.

He strolled around the shop, hands behind his back looking every bit the college professor type. "It's nice. Quite quaint."

The words grated her nerves. He'd always acted as if her business was some type of cute hobby.

When he touched a flower bouquet, she hurried over. "David, why don't we sit down and share a cup of tea? Tell me what you've been up to."

"Sounds perfect. I miss your teas. Nothing quite as good in Butte." He slid a sly glance up her body conveying the double entendre. "No one as beautiful either."

Okay, it was a bit much. While they'd been together, he'd rarely complimented her and even less did he look at her the way he did now. Something was definitely up.

"I can send some back with you."

"You can come with me. I'd love to show you around."

She wasn't about to play whatever game he was trying to pull her into. "I can't, sorry. My boyfriend and I are going away for the weekend."

His eyebrows shot up until almost disappearing into

the creases in his forehead. "What exactly do you mean boyfriend? We didn't agree to date other people. I specifically asked that we take a break, to decide where we'd live."

Whatever conversation he spoke of was not one she remembered. "Nope, that's not how it went. You said you were moving to Butte because you wanted to be closer to your children. I told you I understood and that I was considering moving back here. We didn't exactly speak about the future. It was an unsaid given, in my opinion, that we were parting ways permanently."

He sat back and glowered at her. "Obviously, you didn't waste time moving on."

The nerve of the man. Allison glanced at the door hoping a customer came in so she could keep from yelling at David. "It's been months. Not that I owe you any kind of explanation, but it wasn't planned."

"Seems convenient, you agreed so fast to our separation and moved here only to start dating within weeks. We were together for ten years Allison. How can you just walk away so easily?"

"Hold one damn minute," she said losing her temper this time. "Its obvious by our lack of understanding how we parted that we'd stopped communicating. We rarely did things together. You spent long days at the University. And don't try to tell me it was all work and no play. I know about your little "assistant" Erica." She made air quotes and slammed her hand down on the table.

On her feet now, she waited for whatever he'd say

next.

David narrowed his eyes. "We decided that taking a break could help us work through those things."

"Ha!" Allison interrupted him. "Or did it give you time to see where things went with Erica?" She was on a roll now and by the resigned look on David's face, he knew better than to interrupt. "It's over David. After ten years, I think I know you enough to recognize your version of a booty call. You roll into town to talk about getting back together and I fall into your arms grateful that you've come to your senses. Then we have sex, you stay a day or two and off you go to Butte with promises to call me."

His jaw hardened. "Give me a break Allie. That's bullshit."

"You're right. It is bullshit."

"What's bullshit?" Taylor stood at the doorway and Allison's mouth fell open. She wondered how much he'd heard.

David looked Taylor up and down, not seeming to be at all bothered by the size difference between them. He'd always been of the thought that brains won over brawn and he immediately surmised Taylor to be less than intelligent.

"We are having a private conversation," David started. "If you could please return for your purchase in about an hour..."

"You are not staying that long," Allison said with a roll of her eyes. "Taylor is my boyfriend and he stays."

Nothing in Taylor's expression changed. His hazel gaze was hard and unyielding. It was the first time she'd seen this side of him and understood how criminals must have felt when confronted with the angry cop.

David too stuck up his own ass, decided he could win the standoff. "Well then Taylor, as you may know Allie and I were together for over ten years. As such we have many things that need to be worked out between us. You understand don't you?"

"Yes, I do," Taylor took a step closer and then a second one. Allison tensed hoping he wouldn't deck David. "Ms. Brennan is no longer in a relationship with you. Therefore, if she doesn't wish to continue a conversation, regardless of the subject, or wish that you remain here, you have to leave her property."

At that David was obviously at a loss for words and looked to Allison as if she'd help him.

"Please go David."

With a stiff nod and a glare directed at Taylor, he stalked to the door closing it firmly behind him.

"I'm sorry." Allison let out a sigh. "Not exactly a way to start off our romantic weekend."

"Who said anything about romance?" Taylor pulled her against him instantly covering her mouth with his in a demanding kiss. He pulled back and smirked. "It's going to be hot, sexy and wild. Nothing romantic, no ma'am."

She laughed when he pushed his groin into her. "We're going to get physical."

Over the weeks, he'd become playful and sometimes silly. And after each visit, she'd fallen deeper in love with him.

Allison kissed his throat loving how he responded. "Fine, but if I break out chocolates and roses, you better swoon."

"Hmmm," He responded taking her hand and kissing the back of it. "What was the guy here for?"

She let out a long breath and shrugged. "He tried to say he wanted to explore working things out, but the truth was he was here on a booty call."

Taylor jerked toward the door and Allison was glad David was gone. Tense from head to toe, he narrowed his eyes. "He better not show his ass around here again."

The proprietary side of him was endearing and Allison nibbled at his earlobe. "Or?"

"I'll escort him out of town," he replied with a crooked smile. "You know football extra point style."

"Which leg you kicking with?" Allison said almost regretting the joke immediately.

"Good point." Taylor laughed and both chuckled until a customer walked in.

ALLISON CLOSED SHOP early. Her bags were already packed, so it was but a few moments and they were in Taylor's truck heading out of town. He refused to tell her where exactly they were going and she was fine with it. A weekend away with the man of her dreams was what mattered.

Heck, she would have probably been fine with the Holiday Inn at the next town. Wherever they went, she hoped it allowed for a lot of privacy so she could have Taylor all to herself the entire time.

He glanced at her. "It's about a four hour drive, so make yourself comfortable. We'll stop for lunch in Bozeman."

The trip was something she'd relish for a long time. Between the beautiful scenery of Montana in late autumn and talking with Taylor, she was in heaven.

He told her all about the investigation and how involved he'd been in every aspect of it. There was respect in his tone when he spoke of Captain Morris and it was obvious by the way he described the man's responses to his calls during the job, the man liked Taylor as well.

What also became obvious was how much Taylor missed detective work. It was his calling. Had been his calling.

They drove up a sloping road to what looked to be a huge resort of some kind. A very expensive resort by the landscaping and lush cabins built among trees and other foliage.

Taylor stopped at a grand cabin and looked at her. "Wanna come with me to check in?"

"Yes. I want to see what it's like inside."

"Thought so." He walked around the truck to open her door and they went into what turned out to be a plush and quite formal front office.

A woman looked up from the front desk, her eyes widening just enough to tell Allison she'd noticed Taylor's attractive build. "Welcome to Triple Creek Ranch." She walked around the counter.

"Mr. Hamilton and Ms. Brennan, correct?" She motioned for them to come to the counter.

Allison couldn't help but smile when Taylor took her hand. "Yes. I reserved a one bedroom cabin for three days."

"Here is the key," the woman said, giving Allison a pleasant smile. "There is a list of amenities and activities in the cabin and on screen when you turn on the television for you to take advantage of. Everything on the resort is included."

THE CABIN WAS astonishing. Allison walked from room to room admiring the thick log cabin walls, the impeccable furnishings, and breathtaking art on each wall. The four-poster bed beckoned. With its thick bedding, the scene made her want to yank Taylor's clothes off and drag him into the plushness.

There was a Jacuzzi tub on the private back deck thanks to all the surrounding evergreens.

Three walls in the main room were floor to ceiling windows, which allowed not only for sunlight, but also a way to admire the stunning scenery.

"It's...It's amazing. Oh my God Taylor, this place is so luxurious. I can't imagine how much it cost."

She looked out past trees to a view of a snow-topped mountain. "I don't ever want to leave."

From behind, he wrapped his strong arms around Allison and she relaxed into him.

"Your expression makes the expense worthwhile." Taylor kissed her temple. "Allison, you are very special to me. I wasn't headed in the right direction, but thanks to you, I got my shit together."

She turned in his arms, alarmed at his admission. "What do you mean?"

After a long sigh, he pulled her against him. "I was taking too many pain killers. Was beginning to depend on them. Although I tried to be careful, it was a slippery slope. I won't say I was addicted, but it was pretty damn close."

"Oh honey." She cupped his face. "How do you deal with the pain now?"

His wide shoulders lifted and lowered. "Although some times it hurts like hell, for the most part it's a lot better. I spoke to the doctor about it and he knows that I was headed toward dependency, so he's given me non-addictive alternatives. Hydrotherapy and other stuff works too.

"That's awesome." She wondered how many other things about Taylor she wasn't aware of. Although they spent long times talking, they hadn't been comfortable enough yet to talk about everything.

She slid her arms around his neck. "I love this. Being in your arms and talking."

Taylor kissed her again and both looked to the door when someone knocked. "Must be dinner," he said with a sly smile. "I ordered dinner to be delivered."

The meal was delicious. Tender Beef Wellington, thin green beans and perfectly seasoned new potatoes. They drank red wine as the fire in the hearth crackled, setting the perfect ambiance combined with the candles Allison had packed.

"Why do you keep looking at me like that?" Allison asked, her cheeks warm from his regard. The wine didn't help either. "It's as if you've got something on your mind."

The corner of his mouth inched up. "I like looking at you. You're beautiful. Can't believe that idiot let you go."

Allison's couldn't help rolling her eyes. "I'm not sure why we stayed together so long. We have very little in common and to be honest, I don't think he ever loved me. It was more that we were both comfortable and settled. Should have separated a long time ago."

He nodded. "I get that."

"You ever stay in a relationship too long?" Allison wanted to ask about Felicia, but it was too soon.

Taylor studied her for a moment and drank from his glass. After draining the contents, he poured another and refilled hers. "I need to tell you about Felicia and me." He reached across the table and took her hand.

"She wasn't just my partner."

Allison held her breath for his declaration of being in

love with Felicia.

"Felicia was my best friend. During our years as partners, we spent twelve hours together daily. Every day, day in and day out we sat in a squad car or walked our beat. We knew more about each other than anyone else, I figure." He hesitated. By the pinched expression, he struggled to keep it together.

"Anyway," he continued. "It was hard for both of us after the…shooting. Not only did we suddenly have to spend days and weeks apart, but also then I was medically retired. Now I see what happened, but back then it was so hard. We tried to reconnect the only way it seemed to work. We needed a reason to be together. So…"

Allison wanted to pull her hand away, while at the same time, she needed to hear what came next. "You became lovers," she finished the sentence for him without meaning to.

Taylor nodded. "Yes. Both of us knew it wasn't love. I mean not that kind of love. I am not sure why we did it. Sometimes it felt bad, like as if I was ruining things. We argued one day, just after you moved into town. We finally realized that what we were doing didn't work. So, that is why Felicia came to town often and I went to Billings. We hung out and did things together so that we'd not miss seeing each other so much. I think being partners for so long meant we became co-dependent on one another. Anyway…I need you to understand. Felicia and I were trying to become best friends again."

A tear trickled down Allison's face as she realized how horrible it was going to be for Taylor for a long time. Not only had he lost his children, his father, his marriage, and now his best friend as well. Life had certainly given him a raw deal.

He didn't say anything, but instead looked down to the table. "I hoped you'd understand."

Obviously he mistook her tears for being angry with him. Allison covered his hand with her free one. "I am crying because I hate that you lost your best friend. I am so sorry Taylor. I can't imagine my life without Leah or Tori."

He swallowed with difficulty and attempted at a smile. "Good thing I've got you. Luke, Tobias and Eric too."

"But she was closer to you than any of us. She was your other half in a way wasn't she?"

"What about your mother? Leah told me you keep in touch with her."

Taylor nodded. "I do...did. She'll never get out of prison for killing my dad. Although I felt responsible in some way, it took Felicia's death to make me realize I need to sever all ties with her. I called her one last time to tell her she wouldn't be hearing from me any more."

"How did she take it?"

He gave a one-shouldered shrug. "Frankly, I don't really care. She ruined our family over money. She deserves what she gets."

"Things will get better. I'm here for you. What do

you want to do most? I will do what I can to help."

Instead of a reply, he grinned and blew out a breath. "Let's strip and try out the hot tub."

"Are you serious? It's freezing out there."

"Let's work on you becoming closer than anyone in my life."

The words made her gasp. Before she could recover, Taylor pulled off his shirt and pushed his pants along with underwear off in one fell swoop. "Come on, catch up."

The sight of the very nude well-built hunk walking away made her mouth water.

THE JETS OF the Jacuzzi did a poor job of covering her cries of passion. The combination of cold air hitting her body as she bent at the waist over the side of the tub with the heated water from her thighs down was as exciting as what Taylor did at the moment.

His right hand cupped her sex while he moved in and out of her from behind. His husky grunts in her ear were enough to make her wild.

"Damn you feel so good," his deep words penetrated through the fog of delirium and Allison moaned.

The tempo of his fingers between her folds sent her into a frenzy as she cried out.

MOMENTS LATER WRAPPED in blankets, they sat in front

of the fireplace.

"I think I'm finally beginning to thaw out," Allison said and picked up her cup of hot cocoa Taylor had made. "Not sure I want to try that again."

His warm gaze met hers and he sighed. "Yeah, I think my ass was blue."

"I feel so comfortable with you. It's so strange how well we mesh." Allison looked into the fire and slid a glance at Taylor.

He took the cup from her hands and surprised her by taking her chin and looking directly into her eyes. "I don't think it's strange. We have a lot in common, besides there's something else."

Her breath hitched as she wondered what he'd say. "Like what?"

"I'm in love with you." He swallowed and his brows lowered. "Didn't expect it to happen."

It was endearing how Taylor seemed more pained than happy about the sentiment.

"Oh good!" Allison shrieked and threw her arms around him. "I love you so much Taylor. Have been wanting to ask you how you felt, but was scared of what the answer would be." She pressed kisses all over his face while he chuckled and pretended to protest.

"Don't go getting all mushy." When he cupped her jaw, his words meant little as his eyes shined with emotion. "I am thankful for you Allison."

"Don't make me cry." Allison sniffed and blinked. "You're an amazing man. I hope we spend a long time together."

He nodded and pulled her against his chest kissing the top of her head. "Me too."

AS SOON AS he'd declared his feelings, terror seized him. The urge to leave immediately made it hard to remain calm. Why should he trust that Allison would be with him for a long time? Her words had confirmed his biggest fear.

It seemed fate had decided he would not keep anyone he loved for long. And although a part of him wanted to enjoy the moment, allow the feeling of her returning his feelings to settle in. The other part, the intellectual side, warned of the truth of his life.

"Hey." Allison placed both hands on either side of his face. "What's the matter?" How he loved looking into her green eyes. In truth, he'd fallen for the woman after the first time they'd slept together. Yeah, it sounded shallow, but how they'd connected and how beautifully she made love was the proverbial straw that broke the dam. The dam he'd carefully built to keep everyone at a healthy distance.

"Hey. Look at me," Allison began and waited for their gazes to meet. "Nothing in life is guaranteed. You know this better than anyone. But Taylor, we have to live the life we've got left. No matter if we have months or years left together. I want you to let go of the fear of the "what if". Otherwise I'm going to tickle you until you pee your pants."

She'd accidentally found out he was ticklish and lost control unable to defend himself once someone found the precise spot near his ribs. And of course used the threat of tickling him whenever possible. Just the thought made him tense.

"Don't," he warned. "I mean it."

Allison pulled him closer. "Tell me again how you feel about me?"

"I love you."

The kiss turned hungry and deepened until the hot cocoa, the blankets and his every fear was forgotten. Their entwined bodies confirmed by their declaration were without abandon, as they made love once again.

CHAPTER TWENTY-SEVEN

E RIC PACED AND once again wondered if he'd made a mistake asking Mindy over. He should have offered to pick her up. Or better yet take her out to eat somewhere in town. It was stupid to expect a woman to come to his place on the first date.

Why hadn't Taylor convinced him to change the game plan?

Headlights shined through the window as a car neared and he let out a breath. She'd arrived.

He glanced around the room. The television was on, there was a bowl of popcorn on the coffee table and although dim, the lights were on. He didn't want her to think it was more than what he'd suggested.

Letting out a breath, he smoothed the front of his shirt and went to the door just as she got out of the car. Mindy wore a thigh length red coat sashed at the waist and a matching small red purse hung from her left shoulder.

In her right hand, she held a small bakery box, which

she held up. "I brought a couple of cupcakes. I like sweets when I watch TV."

"Great. Come on in." He moved back to allow her into the house. Once she did, Mindy stopped and handed him the box.

Suddenly nervous like a teenage boy, Eric stood like an idiot unsure what to do next.

"Nice place. It's much bigger than mine." Mindy placed her purse on the closest chair and then removed her jacket to reveal a form-fitting outfit.

And there went his composure. His spit dried up and he fought to swallow.

"Want to put those down?" Mindy asked, her brows coming together in question. "Are you alright?"

"Yeah. Yeah. What movie do you want to watch?"

THE COUPLE ON the television screen was in the throws of making love when the doorbell rang. It was Tori's favorite scene in the movie, when the hero and heroine finally got together after the hero returned from the war.

"Ugh, who could it be at this time of night?" Tori glanced at the time. Ten o'clock at night. Nobody visited that late except maybe Mrs. Clarkson, her nosy neighbor. If that woman's cat ran away again, she was going to scream."

Plastering on a pleasant expression, she peeked out the blinds and immediately scowled.

What in the living hell was Tobias doing there? In the years since he'd moved back, he'd never once came to her house.

Opening the door just wide enough to frame her body, but allowing no more space, she peered up at him. "What?"

The corner of his mouth lifted into a crooked grin. "Hello to you too."

Tori wasn't in the mood for his antics. "It's ten o'clock at night. What the hell do you want?"

"Need to tell you something."

"You could have called."

"You never answer when I do."

"Other than the other night when you called by mistake, you never call me."

"I did. To check on you when your Mom got sick."

"It could have been bad timing and me not recognizing your number. Oh I don't know, maybe I had a moment of amnesia." Tori huffed and rolled her eyes. It was damn cold and the air didn't waste any time penetrating through her socks.

"Come in. It's freezing," she snapped. Once he closed the door behind him, she instantly regretted inviting him in. Tobias had a way of shrinking a room. Without trying, he became the focus of every situation. He was tall, muscular and handsome.

And... he was also an asshole.

To keep from shoving him back out the door, Tori crossed her arms. "Is there some kind of emergency or something?"

"Nah… not really." Instead of standing by the door, he walked around the room, taking in the surroundings. Her dog that'd remained on the couch lifted its head and growled.

"Yeah buddy, I love you too." Tobias ignored the dog's warning and patted its head.

He stopped and whistled when spotting the frozen picture on the screen. "Way to go Tori. I'd never take you for a porn watcher. Good to know you got some kind of something going through those frozen veins."

"Either tell me what you came to say or get the hell out of my house. It's late and I'm tired."

"Mmmm hmmm," he said looking back to the screen. "Yeah, so I don't know why I feel the need to inform you, but I'm going to propose to my girlfriend and would like you to know."

Her stomach sank and knees threatened to give out. It was as if he'd punched her in the gut and Tori was as stunned by the news as she was by her reaction.

"Not sure why you're telling me this."

"Well here's what I've been thinking." Tobias sat down in the same spot she'd been in and once again her dog growled, but was too lazy to leave its bed to bite or something.

Tori refused to sit. She remained standing, and cocked her head to the side.

Tobias had been drinking. Not a lot, but enough to loosen his tongue. He'd always been like that. The reason he rarely touched alcohol was that a person could get anything out of him once he drank more than a couple beers.

"I think," he began again. "That since things between us didn't work out, we have some unresolved issues. That's why we hate each other. I don't know why the first thing that came into my mind once I decided to propose to Mimi was that I should tell you. So I came to town. Was over there at Shooters and thought I may as well get it over with. Come over and fight with you."

"Really, you're marrying someone named Mimi? Why do you think we're going to fight?" Tori challenged. "You said your piece, so you can leave now. No fight."

"Nah," Tobias said. "We are going to fight." He stood and neared.

Tori took a step back. "Not if you leave right now." She pointed at the door.

Instead he took another step closer. "We're either going to fight or we're going to do what that couple on the screen are doing. Your choice."

Her eyes widened.

Was he really proposing sex right after telling her he was going to ask another woman to marry him?

"Get the fuck out of my house moron." Tori gulped when he moved closer and not at all toward the door.

God help her, she was going to let him kiss her.

CHAPTER TWENTY-EIGHT

TAYLOR HOPED TO get to Billings early that Monday morning. The getaway was exactly what he'd needed to help get his head on straight. His plans for the day were made. After one last visit to Felicia's grave to say goodbye, he had two additional stops. One was to see Captain Morrison.

Instead he was at the local café sitting across from his cousin. Eric had called telling him to meet him and then had shocked him silent.

"What do you think?" Eric said.

Jack Garcia, the current Laurel Creek sheriff sat across from Taylor and studied his expression. "I think you'd make the perfect replacement for me."

After discussing a possible move to Billings with Allison, he'd thought the matter of what he'd do with his life was settled for the time being.

He'd been unaware Sheriff Garcia had received an offer in another city, which was too good to pass up. An interim sheriff was needed until the election was held.

Being there was no one interested enough to run, it was a pretty good bet, whoever worked for the six months left in the term would get the job.

Sheriff. Taylor allowed it to sink into his brain. "I'll do it."

"You can think about it," Eric said with a grin. "I mean dude, you've got to talk to Tobias. He'll need to find more help out at the ranch."

"He's already hired another guy. I haven't been much help since my surgery and all."

That he'd planned to go back into law enforcement and this offer came up seemed too convenient. It could be fate was finally giving him a break.

"Sounds like we have a new sheriff in town," Garcia quipped with a chuckle. "Let's get together in my office the day after tomorrow. We'll get everything ironed out. With your credentials, the powers that be will be giddy. Your career runs circles around mine."

The man was good-natured and the local police force of about fifteen respected him. Taylor was honored the sheriff preferred to approach him over the more seasoned officers who worked for him.

"Will there be resentment over this?" He had to ask.

"Maybe," the sheriff was honest. "Only from two. But one is a hot head and the other wouldn't have lasted a month. He likes being out in the streets too much. Being sheriff is sixty percent political and only forty investigative work."

With his injury, Taylor did not aspire to street work.

But having his hand back into investigations and police work, that was the perfect alternative. He didn't have to think about it twice. Besides, it worked best with his plans, not having to commute back and forth from Billings.

ALLISON READ OVER Taylor's text again. He'd gone to Billings and wouldn't be back until late.

He'd been staying at her place since they'd returned from the resort. In many ways they'd become closer there, and although she didn't dare hope, she was already considering what it would be like to be his wife.

Leah strolled in. As usual, the glow of being in a happy relationship emanated from her best friend.

When Luke entered behind her, Allison gave them a questioning look. "What are you two up to?"

"Came to town to get lunch and came to ask you to join us."

Luke went to the display of truffles and glowered. "Are these soaps or food?"

It was strange how differently men saw things. A woman would automatically recognize chocolate in her opinion. "They are chocolate truffles. Wanna try one?"

He shook his head slowly. "I don't think so."

They walked across the street and down another block to a new place, The City Diner. The proprietors, a couple from Oregon, had moved there recently to settle near their married children.

The ambience was comfortable, like that of a diner in a larger town. The name for it was perfect. After ordering salads and a burger for Luke, Leah began talking about joining the local business chapter. "You should do it with me. They need new blood. We need to bring more businesses to Laurel Creek."

"If Taylor moves to Billings, it's going to be hard to make the time. He'll be commuting back and forth and so will I on those days I'm closed."

Her friend smiled widely. "It may all change." She gave the silent Luke a pointed look. "Should I tell her?"

"It's Taylor's job to inform her." Luke seemed relieved when a huge burger was slid in front of him.

"If something is happening to Taylor? Please tell me."

Leah rolled her neck. "Luke's right, I can't. It could be good news or things will stay the same. Nothing drastic. Kinda..."

"I'm going to kill you if you don't tell me." Allison wanted to eat, but nerves made her stomach tight. She peered down at her salad. It looked good.

Her cell phone dinged. It was a text from Taylor.

I have good news.

Coming to get you. I'll be there in an hour.

Allison narrowed her eyes at Leah. "Can you at least give me a hint?"

"Nope. Taylor will kill me and I'm more scared of him than of you."

The aroma of seasoned chicken that was sliced over the bed of artfully tossed spinach reminded her she'd not had breakfast. "Fine. But next time I have a secret, I'm not telling you." Allison forked food into her mouth.

Leah leaned forward. "You better tell me sister. I mean it. If you ever have a secret and don't tell me, I'll call your sister and tell her to come visit."

"That's low."

Luke stood and stretched. "Gotta run and do something. See you in a bit."

Leah smiled and studied Allison. "Let's talk about what's been going on with you and Taylor."

Warmth filled her and it was hard to keep from grinning. "I love him. It's so great. I'm always giddy."

The conversation went on longer than she expected, Leah didn't seem to run out of things to discuss and although she hated not returning to the shop, she loved spending time with her best friend. Then again, she'd be leaving with Taylor once he got there to "pick her up".

It was turning out to be the strangest of days.

Was it going to be their 'thing', Taylor driving without telling her where?

ALLISON SIGHED. "I can't be gone too long. I've already closed the shop for three days for our getaway."

"We're almost there." The truck swayed over the uneven terrain of the dirt trail leading up to the local lookout point.

Allison turned to Taylor. "Seriously? You're taking me to a make-out place? Taylor, although I do think it would be fun, I have too much to do to be coming out here...." She stopped talking at seeing what was usually an open deserted place where teenagers usually parked.

In the clearing stood four men dressed in jeans and matching green shirts. Eric, Tobias, Luke and Ernest also wore identical wide smiles. Each one had a square piece of cardboard in their hands.

"What's going on?" Allison stared at the guys, who didn't move. At the sound of tires she turned to find Leah along with Luke's parents had pulled up next to the truck.

Taylor took her hand. "The guys have something to ask you."

"They do?" Allison frowned at the four men. "What is it?

Eric turned his cardboard to show the word 'Will'.

Tobias' had the word 'You'.

Luke's said 'Marry'.

And Ernest's word was 'Him?'.

Allison giggled, but then gasped when Taylor lowered to one knee. The other women gasped as well. And then it was silent. The only sound was her heart thundering.

Taylor took her hand. "Allison Brennan, I invited important people in my life to be here today as a reminder that not everyone has been taken from me. Will you marry me?" Taylor's voice was gruff with emotion. "I love you with all my heart."

Allison gulped back a sob and nodded. "Yes, I will. Of course I will."

There were high-fives, squeals and clapping as Taylor slipped a gorgeous diamond ring onto her left index finger.

Everyone laughed when Luke and Tobias rushed to help Taylor stand up although he didn't need it.

With only eyes for each other they kissed ignoring the catcalls and clapping.

"I love you so much," Allison said hiding her face in his chest.

CHAPTER TWENTY-NINE

"I STILL CAN'T believe it." Allison sat back on the couch at Tori's place and sipped from the wine glass.

"So where are you two going to live?" Tori asked, her expression soft, but not exactly open. "He still lives with Tobias right?"

Allison sighed. "Most of the time he's at my place. We have a lot to plan. Since he started working as sheriff, he's working long hours every day. Not that there's so much crime, but he likes to greet the second shift and be the one to do the daily briefings for both."

"I can imagine, plus he's probably excited to do what he wants." Tori refilled their glasses. "I'm so happy for you." She held up her glass and they toasted.

"We were going to build a house out there on Taylor's land, but decided with both of us working here in town, it would take too much time to drive that ten miles back and fourth. Especially if he has an emergency." Allison sighed. "So we're thinking of buying the old

Victorian on Oak Street and remodeling it. Not ourselves, but hire someone."

"Good idea," Tori said. "I love that place."

"Where's your dog?" Allison asked. "No yapping today?"

Tori looked down at her lap. "She died in her sleep a couple days ago. I knew she wasn't well, the vet said she was just old. But I wanted to believe she would live forever." Tori sniffed. "I miss my little fur ball."

"Oh honey," Allison said blinking away tears. "I'm so sorry. Why didn't you call me to come be with you?"

"It's been a sucky year. Mom being diagnosed with cancer, Tobias being an idiot and now this. I just wanted to stay in bed and have a pity party."

Allison honed in on the fact Tori mentioned Tobias. "What did Tobias do?"

"Nothing," Tori replied too fast, her eyes sliding to the side. "Just the usual."

Although she'd wondered when to tell Tori, it was a possibility her friend already knew. "So you heard he's getting engaged?"

"Yep, told me himself." Tori let out a huff. "Feel sorry for whoever is marrying the dork."

Allison chuckled. "I have a feeling you're lying. Hmmm." She tapped her chin with one finger. "You're jealous."

"What? No. He's an idiot."

To allow Tobias to marry someone other than Tori was a big mistake. Allison started a plan. She'd speak to

Taylor and Leah. Before Tobias got married, they'd figure out a way to get him and Tori alone. There were some things that needed to be worked out between those two.

OVER DINNER THAT night, Allison couldn't keep her eyes off of Taylor. The top two buttons of his shirt were undone and he was relaxed. The man was sexy without trying.

"What are you thinking about?" He looked up from cutting his chicken. "You've been quiet tonight."

In truth, what bothered her was hard to put into words. "I'm worried about Tori. She's depressed. You know after her mom getting sick and then her little dog died in her sleep the other day. But I'm not sure what I can do for her."

"Is she dating anyone?"

"No. The only relationship she has is with Tobias. They fight all the time."

Taylor chuckled. "Yep, I think it's their favorite hobby. Coming up with creative ways to insult one another."

"We need to figure out a way to get those two alone."

Taylor looked horrified. "Oh no. I'm not getting involved in nothing like that. It's trouble."

"Good grief," Allison huffed the words out. "I have

to think of something. When I do, I'll need your help."

She got up and took their plates to the kitchen sink. While Taylor settled on the couch, Allison went to the bedroom.

"Where are you going so early?"

She turned and smiled. "I've got something special planned for you tonight. Give me ten minutes and then bring your gorgeous self in here."

WHEN TAYLOR ENTERED the bedroom, he found the lights off except for one candle.

Wearing a black see-through teddy, Allison knelt in the center of the bed holding a satin scarf.

"Take you clothes off slowly. I am going to blindfold you."

He was instantly hard. "Yes Ma'am."

THE END

Dear Reader,

Writing is my dream come true, I enjoy sharing my stories with you. Hopefully you enjoyed Taylor and Allison's story. He was a great hero to write and touched my heart with all that he went through.

Can't wait for you to read Tobias' story. Stay tuned for *Ruined: Tobias,* which will be released summer 2018.

I love hearing from you and am always excited when readers join my newsletter list. It's the best way to keep abreast of new releases and other things happening in my world. You can also follow me on Facebook and Instagram.

Newsletter:
landing.mailerlite.com/webforms/landing/t7e4q0

Facebook:
facebook.com/AuthorHildieMcQueen

Instagram:
instagram.com/hildiemcqueenwriter

Email:
Hildie@HildieMcQueen.com

Website:
www.HildieMcQueen.com